The Sword of the Spirits

The Sword
of the Spirits

JOHN CHRISTOPHER

COLLIER BOOKS

A Division of Macmillan Publishing Co., Inc.

New York

Macmillan Publishing Co., Inc.,
866 Third Avenue, New York, N.Y. 10022
Collier Macmillan Canada, Ltd.

The Sword of the Spirits is also published in a
hardcover edition by Macmillan Publishing Co., Inc.

First Collier Books Edition 1976
Printed in the United States of America

Library of Congress Cataloging in Publication Data

Christopher, John. The sword of the spirits.
Sequel to Beyond the burning lands.
[1. Science fiction] I. Title.
[PZ7.C457Sw5]   [Fic]   74-20762
ISBN 0-02-042640-2

With love to SHEILA and JENNY

Contents

Chapter 1   A Traitor Dies   1
Chapter 2   Prince of the Three Cities   23
Chapter 3   Blodwen's Summer   44
Chapter 4   The Player King   65
Chapter 5   The Council of Captains   87
Chapter 6   A Weapon from the Past   115
Chapter 7   The People of the Bells   135
Chapter 8   The Battle of Amesbury   162
Chapter 9   The Walls of Winchester   185
Chapter 10   The Sword of the Spirits   207

The Sword
of the Spirits

1

A Traitor Dies

Less than a week after I was acclaimed Prince of Winchester the pigeons brought a message of defiance from Petersfield.

That city had been taken by my father, Prince Robert. On the advice of the Seers he had kept it, rather than exact ransom as was the custom. He had made one of the Petersfield Captains his lieutenant, but the blue and gold flag of Winchester flew from its citadel.

When my father was killed by treachery and my brother Peter reigned, the men of Petersfield accepted him in turn. He was renowned as a warrior, and had killed the man who killed my father. He ruled both cities, and if there were any in Petersfield who objected they did not do so openly but only murmured in corners.

Then my brother's Lady died, accidentally as it appeared. But when I returned from my journey beyond the Burning Lands to the city of the Wilsh, I found myself accused of her murder. In fact Ezzard the Seer had killed her, by means of the forbidden ancient power called electricity. It was done for my benefit—she was carrying the child who would bar me from succession—but I knew nothing of it.

Nevertheless my brother accused me, along with the Seer and his Acolytes. He ordered me to be burned alongside them in the palace yard. It was then that I challenged him and he accepted the challenge. We fought and his sword broke against mine—that which was forged for me by the Seers in Sanctuary. He flung himself against me, his weapon broken to a stub, and my sword took his life.

So at last I became Prince, as the Spirits had prophesied years before at the Seance of the Crowns. The crowd which had vilified me and shouted for my death cheered me instead. But that was in Winchester. In Petersfield there were other thoughts. I had won some reputation in the north but the news was not yet widespread. They saw me as little more than a boy, a Prince by accident. They thought the time was ripe to regain their freedom.

The message that came was brief and insulting. Michael, Prince of Petersfield, sent greetings to the Prince of Winchester. He would do him no hurt so long as he stayed behind his own walls. And he was sending a gift to help him while away the time there. He was also returning something which had been loaned by his predecessor, for which Petersfield had no further use.

The gift was not long delayed. I was called to the North Gate next morning. During the night the guard had heard the sound of horsemen, but on being challenged they had turned away. These visitors had left some things outside the gate. A wooden sword and shield such as boys use when they play at warriors, and one of those wooden horses that children put between their legs and run with, pretending they are horsemen. There was also the body of Captain Markham, my brother's lieutenant.

A crowd had gathered. They stood in silence. They were looking at the toys and the dead man. They were also looking at me. I saw Blaine and Harding, who had bowed the knee to my father and my brother but been their enemies nevertheless. They had pledged allegiance to me, too, but with the same lying tongues. They would pull me down if they could.

Greene was there as well. He was the Captain who had commanded the expedition to the north. I spoke to him, but loud enough for others to hear.

"Have this body taken up. Tell the Seer he will be buried with full honors in the Captains' graveyard."

Greene nodded. "I will see to it, sire."

"Take up those other things also. Keep them carefully."

He was silent. They were all watching me. I paused before I went on: "We will tie them round Michael's neck before we hang him."

They cheered at that. Greene's face spread into a grin. His fingers rolled the waxed ends of his mustache. As I had learned on the expedition he lacked inner certainty, but he obeyed orders and fought well and bravely. I said: "How long will it take for the army to be ready?"

He said confidently: "They can be ready in three days."

"No." I shook my head; their eyes were on me. "You can do better than that. We ride north tomorrow."

There was another loud cheer, echoing back from the city's walls. I turned and left them.

I talked to Edmund in the little parlor behind the Hall of Mirrors. I sat in my father's old wooden chair, with Margry's painting of my mother hanging on the wall opposite. The morning had been gray, but with mists that were rising now. At times the sun lanced through. It would be hot in the afternoon.

Edmund was my friend, although my father had killed his and taken the crown. He had ridden with me on the expedition; and when my first sword broke in the fight with Peter it was he who had thrown me the Sword of the Spirits so that I could fight on. That sword lay now on a table by the window, unsheathed. Briefly the sun dazzled from the steel.

Edmund said: "It shines brightly."

"Rudi has been putting a polish on it. Hans brought it back to me just now."

Rudi was Master Armorer to the city. He was also a dwarf: armory was one of the trades the dwarfs kept, as an honor as well as a duty. Hans, his son, had traveled with us beyond the Burning Lands.

"A polish," Edmund said, "but not an edge. Even Rudi could not improve on the edge it has."

"No."

The sword was said to have been forged not by men but by the Spirits. I did not want to talk of this to Edmund because even to him I could not tell the truth: I had given an oath of secrecy to the Seers. To change the subject, I said:

"Rudi has been busy with a new sword for Hans. He is determined his son will go into battle as well equipped as any warrior of Winchester, and better than most."

Edmund's hand had been on the sword hilt, caressing it. He turned and said:

"Into battle? You are not letting him ride with the army?"

"Yes. He will ride beside me."

"But it is impossible," Edmund said. "A dwarf may not be a warrior."

"He rode with us to the north."

"As your servant."

"And saved my life when I was a prisoner of the Sky People."

"It was well done," Edmund said, "and you are right to reward him. But not in such a way as this."

"In what way, then?"

"With gold. No dwarf can ever have enough of that."

"This one can. Gold means nothing to him. He wants only one thing: to be a warrior. And he has earned it."

"The Captains will not be pleased."

"They will have to learn to be. Or at any rate put up with it. In the same way that

Greene learned to eat the flesh of polybeasts even though at first it revolted him. In the same way that he learned to accept a polymuf as his equal at the court of King Cymru."

"But we are back in a civilized country, Luke! All that was on the other side of the Burning Lands. We have our customs and they must be kept."

I knew the customs as well as he did. Since the Disaster, when the earth had buckled and belched fire, strange things had happened. Beasts had been born misshapen, and men also. Apart from those of human stock there were dwarfs, who were a true breed, and polymufs, who might have any deformity or crookedness.

Wherever polybeasts were found they were slaughtered, and buried or burned. In the case of children the Seers examined them and made pronouncement, calling them either true man or dwarf or polymuf. Their lives must then be lived in accordance with that decree.

Polymufs were servants always, and could hold no property. They were pitied at best, more usually despised. Dwarfs, on the other hand, worked as craftsmen and were respected as such. They had goods, even land, and polymufs to serve them. The Master Armorer sat at the Prince's table in ceremonial banquets.

All this was according to custom; and custom held also that only a true man could be a warrior.

I said: "I promised it to him. I will not begin my reign by breaking a promise."

"At least put it off for now. Do not take him on this campaign. Wait until things are more settled."

He meant: wait until your position is more secure. I had won my title lawfully and the crowd had cheered me for it. But the crowd was fickle, and not all my Captains were to be trusted. And I was young and inexperienced. I could not afford to make mistakes which in an older man would have been forgiven or overlooked.

I knew all this and understood that he spoke as he did for my good. I looked at him with fondness. He was taller than I and far more handsome; but the long face was frowning, the blue eyes worried. I put my arm on his shoulder.

"Do not fret. They will do as I say as long as I give them a victory over Petersfield. And if I fail they will pull me down whether or not a dwarf rides with the army."

Later that day I saw the new Seer, the one who had been sent to replace Ezzard. His name was Grimm, but it belied him. He was a large and portly man, amply filling his Seer's black coat. He was taciturn in public, as a Seer must be; when he spoke his voice was not harsh like Ezzard's but calm and easy.

I did not see him at the Seer's House but at the palace. By having Ezzard executed I had freed myself of suspicion of complicity in his crime, and the High Seers had confirmed this when they condemned him as one driven mad by false Spirits. But they had agreed that it would be wise for me to seem to stay aloof from the new Seer, at least for the time being. He might come to the palace but I would not go to him, except to a Seance in the way of duty and observance.

Like Edmund, Grimm was unhappy, though not about Hans. He knew nothing of that. It was the campaign that troubled him. He said:

"Luke, it is folly to risk everything at this stage. You need time to consolidate. Things have happened so fast. There should be a breathing space."

I said: "Tell that to Michael of Petersfield. Or to the spirit of Markham, whom we buried this morning."

"He has baited you and you have risen to the bait. It is what he wanted."

I shrugged. "Maybe so. It makes no difference. I could do nothing else."

"You could have laughed it off: the joke was feeble enough."

"And the dead man? Does one laugh off a corpse also?"

"He was not of this city. They could not say his spirit called on you."

"Not of this city, but he served it. He was lieutenant to my father, to my brother, and for a few short days to me. My honor requires me to avenge him."

Grimm scratched his broad white skull, his head being shaven as befitted his office. He said:

"This business of honor wearies me. I hope you are not going to take it too seriously, Luke."

I was aware yet again of the division in my nature and my mind. I knew and understood what Grimm meant. To him and the other Seers such things as honor and glory were of no importance in themselves: they only mattered insofar as they served that larger plan to which their lives were devoted.

The plan was for the renewal of that part of human knowledge which had been abandoned since the Disaster. Those who survived the heaving and twisting of the earth had blamed Science for their miseries. The blame was wrongly placed because the cataclysm had been one of nature, not of man, but the belief was firmly held. In the days after the cities crumbled and crashed, people turned against machines and tore to pieces any who made or used them.

They turned also to a worship of Spirits. These were said to be of two kinds: the Spirits of the dead, and those other Spirits who had never lived in the flesh but who invisibly plagued or benefited men's lives, and served the Great Spirit who ruled and had made everything. In Seances the Spirits talked to the worshipers in darkened rooms, and the Seers presented and interpreted them.

So it was believed. In fact the Seers created the voices, and even the appearances of Spirits, by trickery and the use of those very machines which they claimed to condemn. Their purpose was to gain control of all the civilized lands. When their control was complete they thought they could wean men from superstition and back to science.

But in the civilized lands cities warred against each other, under many different Princes. The first aim of the Seers must be to unite the cities under one ruler. This was the task I had been chosen to undertake. Because of it my father had been made ruler, and after his death I had been smuggled from the city to the safety of Sanctuary where the High Seers lived. Because of it, though without my knowledge or even the knowledge of the High Seers, Ezzard had murdered my brother's wife.

Thus the Seers had gained their first objective. I was Prince of Winchester, a city strong in itself and well placed to conquer others. All this I knew and had accepted and was pledged to serve. But I was moved by other things as well.

I had been reared as a warrior, son of a man who had risen from the ranks and gained nobility on the field of battle. Honor was no empty term to me; nor did it weary me. It was something which had touched my life as long as I could remember. It might mean nothing to the Seers, who spent so much time in trickery and deceit—albeit to a worthy end. But I knew I could not live their way.

I said to Grimm: "Look on it like this. You want me to rule all the cities of the south, in your behalf. My father took Petersfield. Will it do to let that city slip from our grasp?"

"We will get Petersfield back for you," Grimm said. "Only give us time. Trevelyan will see to it." Trevelyan was Seer of Petersfield. "In the short term Michael may hold the city and defy you. But in the long term we shall have him. We opened Petersfield's walls to your father, and we can do it again."

"And will Blaine and Harding sit quietly

here in Winchester while you go about your plottings? They accept me as Prince, but the moment I show myself to be weak or cowardly I will have them at my throat. Have sense."

He was only half persuaded. He said: "We could handle Blaine and Harding."

"So can I," I said. "In my own way."

We rode out next morning into a white mist. One could see no farther than a few yards in any direction. Our progress had to be slow, with our outriders keeping close. We followed the river road to the west, skirting the Downs. It was the longer way, but easier.

Weather had changed greatly since the Disaster. Our seasons were colder than they had been in ancient times, our skies cloudier. This was partly due to the ash flung into the sky from the Burning Lands. There was much rain and periods of settled weather were rare. And when the sun might otherwise have shone, it was as likely that mists would rise from the earth and block its heat.

This happened now. The previous day the sun had burned a path through for a few hours but today the mists were too strong for it. We saw no more than a pale disk at midday. By the time we made camp in the evening the mists were thicker than ever, clammily cold and gray.

Making camp was not easy. Men stumbled over each other and cursed each other's carelessness. And the baggage train, having been hastily put together, lacked certain things. We were reckoning to get our meat from Petersfield farms but we had found no cattle yet. Rations were short: dried beef and bread only.

This and the clinging chill of the mist discouraged the men. I made a round of the camp and found them taciturn and sullen. I tried to cheer them but with poor success. I was not skilled in wooing my fellows and never had been. Their sullenness kindled a similar feeling in my own mind. I tried to master it, and smile and chaff them. But the words and smiles seemed false even to me.

Among Harding's tents I asked if there was anything that was needed. It was a routine question, not expected to be answered, and elsewhere it had not been. But here a man, disguised by the mist, answered roughly:

"If you cannot give us decent food, at least give us Prince's weather."

I did not know how to answer. For that matter I could not tell who had spoken. There was a grumbling murmur from other throats. Then Harding spoke from my side:

"Sergeant! Find that man and bring him here."

His voice was cold and sharp. He himself was a cold, sharp-featured man, slight of body but strong and wiry. He kept good order within his troop. The man was brought to us at once.

He was a man called Morgan. His frame was as large as Harding's was slight. He stood well above six feet tall. There would have been risk of his being called a polymuf giant except that his body was well proportioned. He stood with the Sergeant at his side, looking down on us both.

Harding said: "When your Prince speaks you listen. You do not answer back. I will have no such insolence in my troop. Ten lashes, Sergeant."

The Sergeant saluted. "First thing in the morning, Captain?"

"No," Harding said. "Here and now. In front of his Prince, whom he insulted. And see that they are well laid on."

Morgan stared with silent hatred, but not at Harding. His eyes were on me. I thought of asking for clemency but knew it would only make matters worse. Harding's man had spoken back and it was Harding's right to have him punished.

He was stripped above the waist and made to kneel in front of us. Another soldier stood over him and lashed him. I do not know if the strokes were well laid on, as Harding had commanded, because I did not look at his naked back. I watched his face, staring down at the earth. He took his punishment impassively but on the last few strokes could not help wincing.

Harding said: "Let no other man of this troop shame himself and it by failing to pay due respect to his Prince. It will be fifty lashes next time."

I looked at Morgan's back when they gave him his shirt again. The lash had not broken the skin but there were dark red weals in neat rows. He did not put the shirt on—he would need ointment from the surgeon first—but saluted and walked away.

His eyes looked into mine again before he was lost in the mist. It was Harding who had ordered the lashing, but I who had gained an enemy. Harding came well out of this, I saw. In maintaining his own authority he had filched from mine. They would see me as a boy, Harding as my protector who might, at the right moment, supplant a weakling.

The mist was a little less thick next day and we made more progress. We were in Petersfield lands and for that reason must go warily. Grimm had told me before we set out that the Petersfield army had not left the city—he had the news from their Seer by radio—but they might have done so since. I told Greene to post a double line of scouts.

We came within sight of the city in late afternoon. We showed ourselves but did not approach the walls closely. We retreated into the mist, which was thickening again, and made camp on high ground to the north.

The men were in better heart. We had found cattle which we killed and roasted. We had also found a country alehouse, and the men washed their victuals down with Petersfield ale. They claimed it was poor thin stuff compared with our own, but I warned Greene all the same that the Sergeants must make sure they did not drink too freely. I did not want an army with sore heads if the Petersfield warriors came out next day.

They did not come out, though. The weather had changed. The mist had gone and a fresh wind blew from the north. The sky was cloudy but visibility was good. We made a circuit of their walls. A few arrows hissed through the air at us, falling short. Nothing else happened.

I sent a herald to them in the afternoon. This was according to custom where an army was not already in the field. My message was to Captain Michael Smith. The Prince of Winchester sent him greeting. If he surrendered himself and opened the gates of the city to its rightful Prince, he would have fair trial by the Captains for his murder of the Prince's lieutenant. If not, the swords of Winchester were ready to cut him down, along with any other rebels rash enough to follow him.

The herald was that Captain Barnes who had arrested me at my brother's command on my return from beyond the Burning Lands. He was a tall, thin, gray-haired man, sparing of speech but full of loyalty. He had served my brother and now served me. I could trust him as I could not trust all my Captains.

Returning, he dismounted and his horse was led away, the white cloth of truce blowing from the saddle. I said:

"Well, John?"

The other Captains were present. Barnes said awkwardly:

"I was given a message, sire."

"Tell it, then."

I could have taken him off and got the message in private; but I would not do that. It was plainly an insult. I would receive it publicly.

Barnes said woodenly: "This is the message I was given, sire. 'The Prince of Petersfield bids little Luke go home and play with the toys he sent him. He does not go into battle against children, or those who follow a child.' "

My Captains watched me, from Wilson the eldest to Edmund, little older than myself. Blaine watched from his fat face and Harding from his meager one. Greene put up a hand to twirl his mustache.

I said: "I have heard. Thank you for your office."

I talked to Edmund later. He said:

"He shows himself inferior by refusing your challenge. Everyone must see that."

"Must they? And how will the talk run in th alehouses if we go back to Winchester with our swords still sheathed? That the men of Petersfield mocked them for letting themselves be ruled by a boy. That they judged us unworthy of battle."

"No one of sense will say such a thing."

"I spoke of men in alehouses, not men of sense. And do men of sense sway a mob? They were not men of sense who shouted for my death a week ago."

"You have no choice, Luke, anyway. They will not come out and you cannot make them. Nor can you storm the city. Your father did, but only because they were fool enough to use a machine, which the Spirits caused to blow up and breach the wall. It has been strongly rebuilt and we should have small hope of scaling it."

"He will come out," I said. "I will bring him out."

Edmund shook his head. "How?"

I told him. He listened in disbelief. "You cannot do it."

"You will see what I can do."

I stood with the Captains on a knoll. A little below us and half a mile away were the walls of Petersfield. There was open ground between: grazing meadows and wheatfields. The wheat moved in the wind. I said to Greene:

"Send a squad of men with torches to fire the wheat."

Greene stared, too staggered for speech. It was Blaine who spoke.

"You cannot do such a thing! It is against all custom."

Wheat meant bread for the long hard winter. It stood for life itself. No one rode or fought over growing wheat, and if a campaign ever lasted through summer, harvesting put an end to it.

I said to Greene: "You heard me. That field below us first."

If Greene had hesitated further, the others might have got together and stopped me. As it was they watched in grim silence. There had been no rain for days and the wind had dried the wheat of the mist's dampness. The stalks caught and smoke rolled toward the city.

It was after we had put torches to the second field that they came out. I gave them no chance to assemble in battle array but rode down on them in the shadow of their own walls. We lost some men from arrows but once we had closed the bowmen could not distinguish friend from foe.

I was happy now, feeling the lifting pulse of battle. Hans rode near me, almost of human stature in the saddle, his voice deeply shouting. I saw fat Blaine rise in his stirrups and deal a Petersfield man a blow that almost severed head from body. For all his fatness he was immensely strong. A horseman, a Captain by his blazon, slashed at me. I parried with my sword which, sliding down from his, skinned his arm. I toppled a trooper from his horse with a thrust under the shoulder. Then they were scattering from us and the battle, if one could call it such, was over.

They rode for their gates but we rode with them. We secured the North Gate and after that they were a beaten rabble.

Michael Smith had been a florid flashy man, a good talker who was proud of his voice and given to merry songs at banquets. He sang well even when drunk. But he was not singing now, or talking. His body shivered as Greene hung round his neck the wooden toys he had sent to me in mockery.

I felt sick myself. I had no stomach for watching a man die in cold blood. But I also was being watched, by my own army and the people of Petersfield.

I had been driven to burning the wheatfields, and the trick had worked. It was not so bad to break the rules as long as one won. And ruthlessness followed on from ruthlessness. He had rebelled against his Prince and slain his Prince's lieutenant. He had earned his death. I only wished I did not have to see it.

The day was ending with no sign of the sun. The wind had a cold edge and I could have shivered too, but schooled myself against it.

Greene said in a loud voice: "Let all witness the proper end of a traitor!"

He looked at me. I raised my hand and dropped it. Strong arms pulled on the rope that hung from the pulley of the gibbet, and Michael Smith gave a single gasp as his body was lifted up. His legs twitched as he hung there. They twitched for a long time before they were still.

2

Prince of
the Three Cities

I went to visit Edmund's mother
the day after we returned from Petersfield. I
went unaccompanied and would not let the
man-servant announce me. He was normal in
shape except for a withered arm and had been
in her service for more than twenty years.
When her husband was killed and my father
took the palace he could have stayed there, a
high position for a polymuf, but had chosen
to go with her to the little house in Salt Street
into which she had to move. She was a woman
who commanded affection.

Charles, her elder son, had restored her for-
tunes to some extent, with bounty won in
campaigns under my father and my brother.
She lived in West Street now, in a bigger
house though one still modest for someone

who had been the Prince's Lady. But she had never troubled herself over wealth or display. I found her in the kitchen, baking bread. She held, as few now did, to the old rule that this was something a housewife did not leave to polymufs. And she had trained her daughter, Jenny, to follow the same tradition. Jenny stood beside her at the well-scoured table, her arms like her mother's covered with flour.

Jenny started and looked confused at my appearance. She blushed, and it became her. She had been a plain, thin-faced girl when I had first known her and—an awkward newcomer to the court life which she had lost— had felt the edge of her tongue. She was quite pretty now, especially with her cheeks flushed from the heat of the oven and her present embarrassment.

I said: "You have flour on your nose, Jenny."

It was not true but made her lift her hand automatically to her face. Her nose was floury then. I laughed. She said indignantly, "Oh, you . . . !" then fled the kitchen.

Her mother smiled at me. "Hello, Luke. You come without ceremony and will get none, even though you return as a conqueror."

I took a chair and straddled it. "I am glad to be back."

This was very true. I felt at home in her

house as I did not in the palace. It was a deep thing with me. I had no happy memories of my own home as a child. My mother was beautiful and I loved her, but though she was fond of small animals she did not have the gift of making a child, even her own, feel at ease; and the house itself was badly run. She did not keep her servants long and while they were with her they were slack and sullen.

Edmund's mother said: "Thank you for the roses, Luke."

I had ordered them to be sent down early that morning, the best blooms from the rose garden at the palace. In the old days it had been a great joy to her, and was perhaps the only material thing she missed out of all she had had there. I said:

"Everything in the garden is yours, as I have told you. You are welcome at any time, to pick the blooms or tell old Garnet how to go about his planting and grafting and seeding."

Garnet was the palace gardener, and had held that post through many reigns. He was a polymuf giant, more than six and a half feet tall, and like most such had a weakness of the back. He could no longer stoop but had a boy—a dwarf except that he also had a cast in one eye—who did the stooping for him.

Edmund's mother smiled. "The idea of

telling Garnet anything! But I am grateful for the roses. They have done well this year."

We talked about things of the city: pleasant gossip and without malice. She had no malice in her. She brought me a pot of cider, drawn cold from the barrel, and hot spiced biscuits from the oven. I said after a time:

"Jenny is a long time getting the flour off her face."

"You confused her, Luke." She smiled at me. "She pays attention to the things you say."

I shook my head. "I can scarcely believe that. I have never been a match for her words, nor the cool hard mind that frames them."

"She is not as cool and hard as she seems," her mother said. "It is because they are so strong that she hides her feelings. When she was a child she used to give way to her tempers. Then afterward she was bitterly ashamed of herself. I never punished her for her tantrums; she punished herself more than I could ever have done."

We heard footsteps in the passage, and Jenny came back. She had washed the flour off her face and hands, and had tidied her hair and put a comb in it. I said:

"Well done! That is a great improvement."

Her face was flushed but she was composed. She dropped me a mock curtsy.

"Thank you, sire. It is something to get a word of kind approval from the Prince of the Two Cities.'

I looked at her. Yes, she was quite pretty. I thought of another girl, in a city of gaily painted domes and pinnacles on the other side of the Burning Lands. Jenny was quite pretty but Blodwen was beautiful. And Blodwen, in due time, would be my wife and Lady of this city.

That night we celebrated the victory over Petersfield. The long table was set up in the Great Hall of the palace and I sat at its head. My Captains were ranged on either side down to the first salt. Between the first salt and the second were leading merchants and other men of standing in the city. Below the second salt sat those dwarfs, such as Rudi the Armorer, who were entitled to feast at the Prince's table.

They drank my health, and I gave back the toast, drinking the strong sweet ale out of the Prince's golden pot that stood before me. I was not at ease that night. I drank sparingly, and made an excuse to leave as soon as was decent.

I went out onto the balcony overlooking the palace yard. There was the noise of the banquet behind me, and in front of me but farther off another din. It came from the barracks, where the soldiers were also celebrating. They would be noisier and more drunken than the Captains. I had no appetite for such a scene. I would have preferred to walk alone on the walls and watch the distant glow of the Burning Lands and think of the far northern city of Klan Gothlen. But a Prince had duties, as I already well knew, I resolved to go down to the barracks to greet my warriors.

Since it was a fine night they had brought tables and benches out into the barrack square and were feasting there. The guard at the gate saluted me—soberly, I was glad to see. The noise from the square was much greater now. And I detected a different note in it, of anger rather than rejoicing.

They were so engrossed that they did not see me. They had deserted the tables and were gathered in a corner of the square. Something was going on there. I heard cries, and the clash of swords. I shouted:

"Hold, you fools!"

A few heard me and turned; then others followed suit. They parted their ranks to let me through. These were the spectators. Inside were half a dozen with swords drawn. And backed into the corner of the square a seventh, sword also drawn to defend himself. It was Hans.

I said: "Put up your swords, all of you."

Some of the six obeyed at once, but two hesitated. Hans looked at me and slipped his sword into its sheath. One of the two said:

"Sire, he has wounded one of our comrades —perhaps killed him."

I noticed then another figure who lay groaning on the ground. I knew him: Foster, one of Blaine's men. I said to the man who had spoken:

"Sheath your sword, before I order you a flogging."

He obeyed then, and so did the other. They were both of Blaine's troop. This one was called Sheppy. He was drunk but could talk clearly. He said:

"If we are not to kill him, sire, then he should be hanged. He has no right here, any-way—a dwarf! This is a place for warriors."

The Watch Sergeant had come up by now. I pointed to Sheppy and the others. I said to the Sergeant:

"Arrest these men for brawling. Put them in the cells to cool off."

The Sergeant said: "Yes, sire. And the dwarf?"

Hans looked at me but did not speak. If he were put in the cells with them he would not live till morning. According to custom he had no right here, as Sheppy had said. It was a

place sacred to warriors, and they were entitled to kill anyone who was there unlaw-
fully.

I said: "I will take him into custody myself."

I asked Hans, once we were clear of the
barracks, what had happened and he told
me.

He had gone to take part in the feast, having fought and killed his man outside the
walls of Petersfield. He had been received
with mockery. It was good-humored at first
and he had taken it cheerfully. But Foster, a
cruel man when drunk, had carried things
further. There was a special dance the dwarfs
had at their weddings and celebrations. Foster
demanded that he climb on the table and per-
form this. Hans refused. Foster drew his
sword and said he would prick him on until
he did. At that Hans drew his own sword.
They fought and Hans spitted him. Then his
comrades joined to take revenge. He had been
trying to defend himself against the six of
them when I arrived.

I had listened in silence and was silent still.
Hans said:

"I am sorry, sire." I said nothing. "I should
not have gone there. But . . . they accepted me
in the field, or some of them did. I guessed

there might be hard words but I thought it best to learn to take them."

We had reached the palace. I said: "This needs thought. I will see you in the morning. You are under arrest for brawling, as they are. Do I need to have you locked up, or will you appear on my command?"

"I will always appear on your command, sire."

"Then find yourself a bed in the palace for the night."

I had called a general assembly for ten o'clock. I spoke to Edmund before that. He had heard something of what had happened and I told him the rest. He shook his head, and his face was serious.

"If I may suggest . . . ?"

I gripped his arm at the elbow. "I always listen to you. You know that."

"It does no good to say I warned you there would be trouble. You want to save his life, which they could demand even if Foster does not die. A dwarf in the barracks . . ."

"I made him a warrior."

"Not in their eyes. He rode beside you in the battle. He had a sword and used it. That does not make him a warrior. But I think it will be enough if you now take his sword away. Send him back to Dwarftown and I think it will content them."

"I cannot unmake what I have made."

"Luke," he said, "it defies custom!"

"As the burning of the wheatfields did. As did my father's taking Petersfield and keeping it. There are customs that need to be broken."

"But not this one. A Prince is nothing without his army."

"A Prince rules his army. The army does not rule the Prince."

"A show of strength is a good thing, but one can be too stubborn. Luke, send him back to Dwarftown."

I smiled. "I listen to you, Edmund. But I take my own decisions."

They paraded on the barrack square, each troop behind its Captain and its Sergeants. The men of Blaine's troop who had tried to kill Hans had been brought from the cells and stood there also, but apart. The weather had turned cold in the night. An east wind raised dust from the grounds and even lifted the stiff leather jackets of the Captains. They were at attention and silent. I said:

"There was brawling at the feast last night. Swords were drawn. One of your comrades is wounded."

I paused. In the distance a dog barked, the sound small but very clear.

"I accept some blame for this," I said. "There was one present who was born a dwarf. You will have heard that he served me well in the expedition to the north. You have seen that he fought at my side before Petersfield. But it might be said that saving a Prince's life or fighting in one of his battles does not make a warrior."

I let them wait again. I saw the faces of my Captains: approval in Edmund's, the twisted beginning of a smile in Blaine's. I said:

"Warriors must obey their Prince but he has a duty also: to make his will clear. This I shall now do." I raised my voice: "Hans, son of Rudi!"

He came from the shadow of the gate where I had stationed him. He walked steadily forward. He was tall for a dwarf but he had a dwarf's rolling gait. There could be no mistaking what he was. He stood before me and saluted.

I said: "Do you wish to serve me and this city as a warrior?"

"Yes, sire."

"Do you accept the duties and the dangers, and will you obey all the commands of your officers?"

"I will, sire."

"Then be it known that by my command this man is a warrior. From this moment he is your comrade. Captain Greene!"

Greene took a step forward and saluted me. "Sire!"

"Will you accept this man in your troop?"

His face showed nothing. He said:

"I accept him, sire."

"As to the brawling . . . I accept some blame but punishment is required. We draw swords against the city's enemies, not each other. Apart from Foster, all who took part will be confined to barracks for a week. You may dismiss the men, Captain."

I waited until they had broken up. The six of Blaine's troop and Hans were taken by the Sergeant of the guard for fatigue duties which were part of their punishment. I saw the anger in Sheppy's face as Hans joined them, and his lips moved: in a curse, I guessed. There would be plenty of cursing and jeering during the week to come. But Hans was one of them now, and they would do him no harm. Their own lives would be forfeit if they did.

It would be hard on Hans; but he had chosen to be a warrior and a warrior must learn to bear hardships.

Edmund came up to me at last. He said:

"Well, you did it." There was unwilling admiration in his voice. "But I still think you were unwise."

"I know that." I grinned. "It is a cold morning. Come to the gymnasium and we will wrestle a little warmth into ourselves."

Winter closed in early, with a blizzard that blew for four days and left snow drifting six feet deep in the High Street. There was a thaw after that, but a few weeks later the snow returned and this time stayed.

Life was more confined but had its pleasures. For the boys there was skating on the river by the grazing meadows, the snowball fights that raged right across the city and did not always respect the dignity of older people, toboggan races on hard-packed frozen snow down the High Street. For the rest there were the entertainments of jugglers and minstrels, dancing and feasting and talk. Winchester was prosperous, her silos and granaries full, her farms stocked with fat cattle. We were well prepared for the hard months.

But there was work as well as pleasure. Rudi and his dwarfs labored in the Forge. With Greene I made a close inspection of swords and armor and rejected any that was worn or faulty. And I had the Captains keep their troops long hours at drill. I increased their rations of meat and ale to make up for this. There was some grumbling but they went at it willingly enough for the most part.

My life was full, with the army and the court. At times, though, I got away on my own. I walked one day on the walls, with no one near me. The sky was largely clear for once, sharp blue with white clouds and that darker one that always rested on the northern horizon, where the Burning Lands smoked and smoldered. I thought of the journey we had made through the pass that ran across them, and I thought of King Cymru of the Wilsh, and his daughter Blodwen.

I was not far from the North Gate. Snow had fallen in the night and only my footsteps had disturbed it here. I turned and saw a figure farther along the wall, coming my way. There were steps near and I thought of going down into the city to avoid him. Then I saw it was a black-cloaked Acolyte, and recognized Martin.

I greeted him as he came up, and said:

"What brings you here?"

"The same as you, sire, probably: an urge for solitude."

I took his arm. "No 'sire,' Martin. We are still friends, I hope."

He smiled, and his face lost the tense worried look that it often bore.

"I hope so, too, Luke!"

I had seen little of him since becoming Prince. As boys he and Edmund and I had been companions, but life had taken us along dfferent paths. Edmund was a warrior and one of my Captains, so our ways lay much together. But Martin had become an Acolyte to the Seer. This would anyway have limited our companionship; my wariness of being associated with the Seer and the Seance House only made it more certain.

Now as of old we walked and talked together, and I realized how much I had missed him.

We looked over the snow-covered roofs of the city. In the distance I saw the Seance Hall, and the Ruins beyond it. The Ruins were the great mound of stone beneath which lay the small underground room in which we three had met as boys, to talk and plan in secret. I pointed to it, and said:

"Did you know the Christians seek our old playground?"

"For what?"

"Peter gave them gold for a new church when he used their secret tunnel to get back into the city and surprise the Romsey men who had captured it. They have not built it yet. They ask for that land to put it on. They say there was a great Christian church there in ancient days."

"What did you say to them?"

"I told the priest I would think about it."

"Will you say yes?"

"I think I will. The first debt was paid, but there was a death after that. Ann, my brother's wife, was a Christian. It would please her Spirit. And the ground is of small value. No one else will build there, out of superstition."

Martin shrugged. "They are mad, but they do not do much harm."

"There is more to it than building. They are bringing their Bishop from Oxford."

Each set of Christians has its priest as a leader, but there was only one Bishop in the civilized lands, who ruled them all. I said:

"It is a compliment, I suppose. They recognize the supremacy of our city. It is strange, though, that they should bring him to the seat of power and riches, when they claim to despise such things."

"They would probably say power and riches are good when they are means to a good end: to guide men's minds to what they think is truth."

"You are generous," I said. "It is a vastly different truth from the one you seek, after all. They have no interest in Science. What they call truth is a god who walked as a man, who died an ugly death, and raised himself from the dead afterward."

His smile returned. "They will not win over any but madmen like themselves with such stories."

"And polymufs," I said, "whom they flatter by letting them join with them as equals."

Martin nodded. "A shocking thing, that. As shocking as turning a dwarf into a warrior."

He smiled again and I was glad to see it. I punched at him, as we had done when we were boys.

"That is by the Prince's will," I said. "Remember it, Acolyte!"

Winter ended at last and it was spring again. There was the Contest of the Young Captains, in which I had won the jeweled sword and started on the path which led to my becoming Prince. This year it was very one-sided. Isak, the youngest son of Harding, was the winner, gaining his victory without losing a man.

Spring turned to summer and I took the army out on its campaign. We rode south this time, down the valley of the Itchen. There was a score that needed settling with James of Romsey whose father, Fat Jeremy, had treacherously killed mine.

I expected wiles rather than courage from

him and was not disappointed. He brought his army out of the city on our approach but on the far side of the river which runs through it. From there he fenced with us, defying us to cross and ready to strike if we did so.

This continued for two days of warm cloudy weather. Then at the close of the second day the clouds rolled away. And that night, the air being calm and still, mist rose from the river and spread out over the fields in which we were encamped.

In the morning the mist remained, thick and white, blanketing and disguising everything. A brightness in the east marked the position of the sun, but there was no sign of it breaking through. The hours wore by slowly and we could do nothing else but hold our ground. Not until the afternoon did the objects round us start to take shape, as the brightness overhead focused into the silver and then golden disk of the sun. The mist lifted, and as it did the Romsey army launched itself on us.

James, though not much older than myself, was known for his cunning, and the attack had been well planned. He had taken advantage of being on familiar territory. He had brought his army quietly across the river by a ford north of our position, and then as quietly led them down to a point within striking distance. So he could attack with the lifting of the mist and take us by surprise.

This is what happened, and for a time our men were confused and fell back. But they had confidence in themselves from past campaigns and the winter's drilling had toughened and instilled discipline in them. The Captains rallied them and they fought savagely.

It was a battle fought on foot. They had left their horses on the other side of the river and our own, of course, were still tethered. It did not last very long. James had used cunning in the preparation and no doubt would have done well chasing a beaten rabble, but he had little stomach for an enemy that took his charge and fought back. He ran, and his men, left leaderless, ran also. The mist was rising all this time. They ran north along the river bank and were in full view. We untethered our horses and mounted and rode them down. We had them at our mercy and they surrendered. They could do little else.

We took all except the few who had run first and escaped across the river. James had been one of these. When their Captains surrendered a gray-haired man spoke for them. He said:

"This ransom will not be easy to pay. Will you give us time, sire?"

I said: "There will be no ransom."

My own army and my Captains stood behind me. The Romsey Captain said:

"No ransom?"

I said: "My father took Petersfield, and I take Romsey. You belong to our realm of Winchester. Serve it faithfully and you will come to no harm."

There was silence before the Romsey Captain spoke.

"Maybe the men of Petersfield did not set a high value on their ancient liberties. We do. Prince, you cannot ask this. We have lost the battle and will pay you ransom. But we will not serve you, nor your realm."

The silence came back. So short a time before there had been the clang of metal, cursings, men shouting and dying. The last shreds of mist steamed off the river. My men listened as closely as theirs. I said:

"You speak like an honest man. You could have given me soft words and defied me later. And I would have been forced to come again to your city, this time in anger. But since you defy us now you will return to your city weaponless. And we will keep a garrison there as long as it is needed."

He stared at me. "You are not in the city yet."

"No." I nodded. "But will the gates be kept

shut against us, with so fine a crop of hostages?"

He bowed his head, in acceptance. It was all silence, and their defeat spoke louder than our victory. I said to Greene: "See to it," and rode away.

We left our garrison in Romsey and rode back along the Itchen valley. Citizens crowded out from the South Gate, cheering and welcoming us back. They shouted my name: "Luke!" I heard them cry: "Prince of Three Cities!"

I rode at the head of my army into Winchester. The crowd was even thicker inside, and noisier. Then it seemed to melt and grow quiet. I saw horsemen with foreign but familiar trappings. And someone else.

She sat white-robed on a white horse. Her beauty seemed to make the air grow still. She bowed her fair head, her blue eyes smiling.

She said: "I grew tired of waiting, Luke. So I came to see this city which you promised me."

3

Blodwen's Summer

It is strange what power beauty can wield over men's minds. Blodwen had been only three days in the city, but she had conquered them absolutely.

They cheered us as we rode up through the streets together to the palace. Then they gathered outside. This was usual after a victory. The Prince must show himself on the main balcony, to be cheered again and to promise his citizens free ale at the victory feast that followed.

They acclaimed me well enough when I went out, and shouted my name with vigor. But when I drew Blodwen out to stand beside me, I thought they would go mad. I had never heard such cheering anywhere. And when she

blew them a kiss I thought they were mad
already: the din battered one's eardrums.

And her power, I saw, lay not in her beauty
alone but in the warmth and ease that went
with it, that were a part of it. The gesture of
blowing them a kiss illustrated that. In the
press directly under the balcony I saw an old
polymuf road-sweeper called Dirk. He was
not much of a sweeper, having arms little bigger than a baby's to hold his broom, but there
was no other work he could do: his mind was
not much greater than a child's, either. He
stood and held up his tiny arms toward her,
and tears flooded down his face unchecked.
He had taken the kiss as his; as they all had.

I looked at her, close by where they were
far off, and still found no flaw. The pink and
white of her skin, the delicate gold of her
hair, were without blemish, as was the wide-
eyed candor and radiance of her look. I
thought of my own roughness beside her: no
one could ever have praised me for my looks.
But at least this beauty was to be mine, and I
had a right arm strong enough to defend it
against all threats or dangers.

It took some doing but we escaped from
them at last. And at last we were alone, in my
parlor. She said:

"I like your city, Luke, and your people."

"It is plain they love you."

Now that we were together and on our own I felt my old awkwardness with her return. It was part of the awkwardness I had always felt with girls, but made worse by the power her beauty had over me, too. I had a strong arm to defend her, but I wished desperately for a readier tongue with which to talk to her.

She smiled. "You have not given me much welcome yet. Are you not glad to see me?"

She offered me her cheek, and I kissed it clumsily. Then I wanted to take her in my arms and kiss her again, but she slipped from me. I said:

"I am very glad to see you. You know that. But astonished. How do you come to be here?"

She shrugged. "As you came to my city— through the wild country and over the pass between the Burning Lands." She gave a small shiver. "That was the part I did not like—those smoldering black rocks and sand, and no life anywhere."

I burst out: "But how did your father permit it? To make such a journey and take such risks . . ."

Blodwen smiled. "As I told you in Klan Gothlen, we women of the Wilsh are our own mistresses. We are not so easily bid as your southern ladies. My father did not want me to come but he did not try to stop me. He sent fifty of his finest soldiers to guard me, though. I was safe enough from the savages."

I could believe that: every one of the fifty would have given his life for her, and although at first I had been contemptuous of the Wilsh as soldiers I had reached a different view before we left their city. But I was still astonished that she should have come. Not only because of the hazardousness of the journey. There might also seem to be impropriety in it. It was not fitting for a girl, even though betrothed, to seek out and visit a man.

She smiled at me again, and I reminded myself that these considerations were part of our southern customs. And I realized that even if that were not the case, even if such rules bound girls in the land of the Wilsh as well, they could not bind Blodwen. Nothing could. She did not live by the rules of others but framed her own.

She said: "I will tell you why I came, Luke —apart, of course, from wishing to see you again."

She laughed at those last words, making a jest of them and taking away, though gently, some of the pleasure they had given me. She put her hand on mine, and I felt its soft warmth.

"Do you remember," she asked me, "when

we spoke on the stairs above the throne room in my father's palace?"

"I remember."

"And how after faithfully promising to return one day and claim your prize"—she laughed again at this—"you asked me if I would rather you did not?"

I nodded. She went on:

"I thought a lot about you after you had gone, Luke. You came to our land as a stranger and stayed as a hero. The artists are hard at work on the painting of Luke and the Bayemot. The great Gwulum himself is painting the figure of Luke because he cannot trust any of his disciples to do it well enough. It was a strange and dazzling time, your stay with us."

Strange and dazzling for me also, but I said nothing.

"You had said you would return, and I think you are a man who keeps his word. But your return must be for one thing: our marriage. From that must come a shared life together, a real thing, not a dream. And for me a life in an unknown land and city, since a wife must go to her husband's country.

"So I resolved to come and see that country first, and to see you in it. Not Luke from beyond the Burning Lands, Luke the Slayer of the Bayemot; but Luke of Winchester and in

Winchester. My father promised me to you and he too keeps his promises. But I know you would not yourself hold me to a promise to which my heart gave no assent. So I have come to see, before any irrevocable step is taken, the place where I might live and, I suppose, die at last. And the man with whom that life might be spent."

She had said this last with a serious face, in no jest but in earnest. I knew she meant it. The awareness struck into me, almost with the cold bite of steel, that I was not sure of her. Her coming here was evidence of that: not reassurance but its opposite.

I suppose my face showed something of my feelings. She said:

"Cheer up, Luke! We are neither of us likely to die just yet. And it gives you the chance to think again as well. I would not hold you to your word, either."

I said, stammering: "You . . . do not need to."

"Don't I?" She looked at me, amused. "You would make a poor courtier, Luke. But being a Prince you have no need to play that role. And I am glad of it. We have glib courtiers enough in Klan Gothlen. You are a warrior. Now, tell me about all your battles and victories."

When Edmund joined us he took her hands and kissed her on the cheek as I had done. I was glad to see them so pleased to see each other. They fell to chattering at once, about people we had known at the court of King Cymru. I recalled them well enough myself, but had nothing to say of them.

She had no warning to give to him, of course, so there was no shadow of seriousness and therefore less constraint. In fact his presence made things easier for me as well. I could relax, listening to them talk. I did not have much to contribute, but it was enough to hear them.

Edmund spoke of the banquet which would celebrate her coming. She said eagerly that she loved banquets; she wished it were this evening instead of the next day. Edmund chaffed her, saying it was her vanity that prompted the wish: to sit at the head of the table and see the eyes of all Winchester's Captains engrossed with her beauty.

She tossed her head. "I am not so vain as to think your Captains must look at me in preference to your own ladies."

"Perhaps they would not if they had a choice. But since you will be the only lady present, at whom else should they look? At each other?"

"The only lady present?" She looked at me.

"Surely not! Your ladies will not refuse to greet me?"

"No," I said, "but it is not our custom to have ladies at our banquets. That was something we found strange in your city."

"Can you not change your custom?"

"It would not be easy."

Edmund laughed and we both looked at him. He said:

"I was thinking of another custom that one would not have thought it easy to change—of the Prince who turned a dwarf into a warrior!"

"What is this?"

He told her the story of Hans. She listened and turned to me.

"There, Luke! If you can break one custom you can break another."

"It is not the same thing."

"In what way is it different?"

I tried to explain, but stumbled over my words. One was a question of making good a pledge, of honor. No question of honor was involved in the other. Custom must hold except under a stronger compulsion.

They contested me eagerly, stumbling not over their own words but each other's in their anxiety to prove me wrong. They were both much readier tongued than I was, and their combined attack, with Edmund reinforcing

Blodwen and Blodwen putting Edmund's argument again but more sharply, overwhelmed me. I did my best, doggedly, to maintain my stand.

Edmund said, laughing: "The one thing he really believes in is the Prince's will. This Prince's will, anyway! He will break the customs he wants to break, and nobly uphold the rest."

"The Prince's will, indeed!" Blodwen said. "And what of the Princess's? Does my will count for nothing?"

"Not against this tyrant," Edmund said. "But if you beg it of him prettily, he may grant it you as a favor. It is worth trying."

They were both laughing. In mock humility Blodwen dropped to her knees and bowed her head.

"My Lord," she said, the tone piteous, "will you grant your handmaiden, out of your greatness and nobility, this humble plea?"

I lifted her to her feet, laughing myself. "You will soil your gown."

"Not in Winchester," she said. "Your floors may be of plain wood but I notice they are well scrubbed. Well, Luke?"

"You can have your way," I said, "though Strohan, my butler, will very likely die of shock when he hears. The ladies will be at the banquet."

"Good!" she said. "I look forward to seeing them. I think a man may be well judged by his lady. I am anxious to see Edmund's."

"I have none," he said.

Her eyes widened. "Not even one in prospect?"

"I have been kept too busy by Luke, what with expeditions into the barbarous north and battles against the city's enemies."

"But you must bring someone, now that the great Prince has given way to us!"

"I can bring my sister, I suppose."

"Then do so! A sister may tell one something about a man as well. Perhaps more than his lady could."

I watched them and was happy. I did not mind being bested in such a thing as this and by such a pair: my betrothed bride and my best friend.

She could charm anyone when she set out to. I need not have worried about Strohan; he was already her besotted slave. The banquet was a great success and so were all the other receptions, whether at the palace or in visiting the city's nobles. People opened to her, like flowers to the visiting sun.

And since she was not one of those who put on a show, of ceremony or graciousness, she was as winning in small intimate gatherings as in more formal ones. She was interested in the diversity of mankind, and loved to hear men talk of their ideas and beliefs. With Blodwen to draw them out, they talked readily enough.

She said one day something about asking someone to join us for supper in her apartments and I nodded absently. My mind at that time was preoccupied with a captaincy that had fallen vacant and the various claims of those who should be considered for the place. She said:

"I must make inquiries in case there are things he cannot eat. In my country the Christians do not eat meat on one day in the week. They may have some such rule here also."

"Not eat meat? But if they are Christians I suppose it does not matter: they do not have to swing a sword." I realized, belatedly, what she had said. "But you are not asking Christians to dine here?"

She said, scolding: "You have not been listening to what I said. Not just Christians. Their Bishop."

"But you cannot do so, Blodwen," I said. "I know little of the Christians in your country, but here they are despised and rightly. They are a crazed lot, always talking about this dead god of theirs. They were useful to the city once, when Peter led the army through their secret tunnel, but that has been well paid for. Not only in gold, and now in land, but also in boredom during the time my brother was Prince and they had access to the palace."

"He is not being asked to the palace," she said, "but to my apartment as my guest." I shrugged in resignation, realizing that her mind was made up, and she smiled at me. "You will come, won't you, Luke? I have asked your friend Martin as well, so you can talk to him if the boredom proves too great."

"Martin! But he is an Acolyte. You cannot ask him to meet a Christian."

She smiled again, very sweetly. "I have already done so. And he has said yes."

I had seen the Bishop once or twice in the city. Even apart from the black gown he wore and the wooden cross he hung around his neck, he was distinctive in appearance. The priest who counseled Ann and consoled Peter after her death had been a small, weak-looking creature with a stoop. The Bishop was big and broad, with powerful arms and hands and a strong wide face. Like the priest his head was shaved except for a thin circle of hair above the ears, but his huge skull had such a polish on it that I doubted if any hair grew there in the first place.

His voice matched his frame, being deep

and booming. He spoke as someone sure of himself, and laughed readily. And however he may have behaved among his lunatic followers, with us he talked in a rational fashion. He spoke of the city, which he said he had long wished to see, and told us things concerning its past, before the Disaster, which were new to me. I had learned from the Seers that there had once been kings and queens in the great city called London, who had ruled all England and territories beyond the oceans as well. The Bishop told us that in still earlier days English kings had ruled not from London but from this city of Winchester. It may have been no more than a fanciful tale, but he told it convincingly.

He did not say anything about his Christian god until Blodwen put questions to him, but then he told that tale well also. It was the wildest fantasy, this story of the maker of the whole universe being born in a stable, living as a man and dying a painful and degrading death, but he described it so well that for the moment one could almost believe it.

But Martin said: "You have not told all, Bishop." There was anger in his voice. "You have not spoken of his mother being a virgin, or a star moving through the sky to lead kings to worship him."

The Bishop said: "These things are less important."

"Are they? Your Christians do not think so. Nor do I. Truth does not surround itself with lies."

"You speak warmly, Acolyte," the Bishop said. "You are a devotee of truth?"

"I know of no better thing to seek."

"And do you find it in the darkness of your Seance Hall, when the Spirits speak with the tongues of men?" His voice was amused, and I saw Martin's face flush. "But let us keep to abstract matters. There was a poet in ancient days who wrote about truth. He said:

'Beauty is truth, truth beauty. That is all
 Ye know on earth, and all ye need to know.' "

Martin stared at him. "It is well said."

"Well said, but he gives himself the lie. His words are beautiful but they are not true. Truth can be ugly."

"I deny that!"

"Do you? Listen. A good woman lies dying. She asks after her son. The truth is that he is a convicted felon and will be hanged in the morning. Will you tell her so? Truth which lacks pity is a cruel thing, and where there is cruelty there can be no beauty."

Martin said: "The poet spoke of the nature of things, not of men's speech."

"Is not men's speech part of the nature of things? What men do matters more than what they know. Our ancestors had wonderful machines." I started at that word; even to use it was improper. "Men turned against them because it was machines, through the agency of evil spirits, that caused the Disaster."

The Bishop smiled. "At any rate, that is what the Seers tell us. I am glad myself that the machines are gone but for a different reason. Machines put a distance between men. A man could give an order on one side of the world and command obedience on the other. Our Prince here must earn obedience, from men he sees and who see him. In those days a man could press a button and kill a thousand men a thousand miles away. We Christians, as you know, do not accept any kind of killing, but if killing there must be I would rather it were done by a warrior who kills with his own hand, and knows what bloody corpse he leaves behind."

I did not like this talk of forbidden things. I would have ordered him to be silent, even though he was a guest of Blodwen's, but she herself spoke first. She said:

"The old days are dead and gone and it does no good to talk of them. And of course you are right, Bishop, to say that one does not

tell harsh truths to someone not strong enough
to bear them. But it is a better case when
people have that strength."

"It may be better," the Bishop said, "but it
is not a common thing."

"Not among your Christians, maybe," I
said.

He shook his head. "Not even among warriors."

They were good days, passing lightly and
quickly. I forgot the doubts which Blodwen's
words had put into my mind on that first evening in the palace. And she did not speak in
such a way again. If she had seemed unhappy
I might have been troubled. But she was content, and that contented me.

I remember a day in high summer when we
went in boats on the river. There were no
more than a dozen of us in the party, all
young. We went down river, scarcely needing
to row because the current took us. It was a
fine morning, the sky blue and white, the sun
hot when it pierced the clouds. We went a
long way, past Twyford, and on to the place
where the river meanders through a broad
valley of water meadows.

We picnicked there and then lay idly on
the grass of the river bank, the boats moored

and bobbing beside us, and talked and
laughed and were pleasantly idle. We were on
our own, with no servants even, and I could
lay aside the cares and countenance of a
Prince. Apart from Blodwen there were three
other girls, one of them Jenny. They were
pretty enough in their summer dresses. But
compared with Blodwen they were daisies to a
rose.

Her dress was green, with long full sleeves.
It was a Wilsh cloth, more brightly hued than
any we had in the south. Its brightness made
the grass look dull, as her beauty made the
other girls seem plain.

We had no minstrels either, but Edmund
and Matthew Grant had brought their lutes.
They played them for our amusement, and
Edmund sang. He had a good voice, high but
sweet and true. One of his songs was "The
Miller of Dee," and Blodwen, applauding it,
said:

"We have that same song in my country! In
fact it is said that he lived beside the river
higher up the valley in which Klan Gothlen
lies. It is called the Dee."

Edmund laughed. "And do you have this
song also?"

His fingers plucked the strings in a slow
haunting tune. He sang:

"Oh Greensleeves was all my joy,
Greensleeves was my delight,
Greensleeves was my heart of gold,
And who but Lady Greensleeves?"

She clapped her hands and said: "I have heard it, but never so well sung, I think. You should be a minstrel, Edmund."

I laughed. "I cannot spare him, though! I have more need of him as a warrior."

It was not long after that the cares of state caught up with me again. Horsemen came riding toward us along the river bank. It was Greene with a small troop. The pigeons had brought word from Romsey: there was trouble there. It had been put down and the garrison was in no danger, but Greene had thought it best to tell me.

He had had the sense also to bring a spare mount. We were almost as near Romsey as Winchester. I said:

"We had better ride over and make sure."

Blodwen protested: "Do not spoil such a day as this, Luke! He has told you there is no danger."

I hesitated, but said: "No, I must go, my love. There will be other days to enjoy. Edmund will row you back for me. Will you not, Edmund?"

"As my Prince commands," he said, "though I would point out that it will be against the stream. I shall expect a good wage for such heavy work."

We laughed, and I said to Blodwen: "Give him his supper, and a pot of ale to cool him."

"You will not be back this night?"

I shook my head. "I think not. But tomorrow, certain."

I looked back as we rode away. Blodwen sat with her knees drawn up and her small hands clasped over them. Edmund stood by her, playing the lute and singing. It was a fine scene and I was reluctant to leave it. But as I had said, there would be other days.

Martin came to see me in the palace one night a few weeks after this. He wasted no time, but said:

"I have come to say good-by."

"Good-by!" I was astonished. "You are not leaving us?"

He nodded. I thought how absurd he looked with his tonsured head and spectacles above the Acolyte's black cloak. It was hard to believe that he had once fought at my side in the Contest. But despite the absurdity, perhaps because of it, I felt an uprush of affection for him.

I said: "To go where?"

"To Sanctuary."

"But for how long?"

"I don't know. Perhaps for good."

"You cannot do that, Martin," I said. "Visit your High Seers, if you must, and see their wonders. But then come back to me. They can offer nothing to make up for having to live underground like a mole, with neither sunlight nor fresh air." I spoke with more confidence, remembering my own time in Sanctuary and how I had chafed against its confinement and restrictions. "You *could* not do it. It is different for the High Seers. They are old men but you are young."

"I cannot stay here. I cannot go on with the trickery and deception and lies in the Seance Hall. The end may be good but I cannot tolerate these means. That Christian Bishop mocked me for it and I had no answer."

I said: "He will bear watching, that one. He knows too much and speaks too freely. I have warned Grimm of it. But if this is all your problem, it is easily solved. I told you once before I could rid you of that black dress if you wished. It is still more true now. I have only to say a word to Grimm and you are dispensed from the vows you took."

He smiled, but with no joy. "And what shall I do then? I am no warrior and would prove a poor courtier."

"You can be my friend and counselor, as you were when we were boys together. If you desire an office I can call you Chancellor, as Cymru calls Snake, the polymuf who advises him."

"And if I advised you to give Petersfield and Romsey back to their citizens? You need no counselor, Luke."

"I need friends."

"It is no good. Not much more than a year ago I hung in chains, with faggots round my feet, and men with torches ready to light them. You saved me, but it marks one to watch a hard and ugly death draw close. I must do something with the life you gave back to me, and it is not enough to sit at court and be your friend."

I could not follow his thoughts. A man faced death, but when death drew back forgot it until the next time. But there was a desperation in his face. I felt suddenly cold. I had friends already, and Blodwen, but I did not want to lose him. Yet I would make no plea. I said:

"So be it. The Spirits go with you."

4

The Player King

At the time of the Autumn Fair, with the campaigns over and the fields harvested, we held a great ball in Blodwen's honor. I sent the pigeons far and wide and got fair answer. The Princes of Guildford and Basingstroke, Alton and Andover and Salisbury came to us as guests. Strohan was in desperation, finding room for them all in the palace. And the Prince of Oxford sent his son.

Oxford was a city of great power and influence, ruling much territory. Towns as remote as Marlborough, more than thirty miles away across hilly country, stood under its sovereignty. The Seers must have thought of this city before they chose Winchester as the pivot of their plan. I guessed that their reason for rejecting it was because it lay remote, on the edge of the civilized lands, while we lay at the heart. Their northern border was the Burning Lands. Under that smoking sky, livid with flame by night, they were remote in a different sense: they were a sullen people, content to keep to themselves. Probably that was another reason why the Seers had looked elsewhere.

Our armies had never met theirs in the field, and there had never before been a royal visit. I knew why this invitation had been accepted. I ruled three cities now from Winchester. Even in the remoteness of Oxford that was something to cause sober thought. The Prince had sent his son to take a close look at me and my city.

I was prepared to be treated warily, and to treat him warily in return. He was a few years older than I, and had been heir to his father's throne all his life. I expected an aloof unfriendly man, mindful of the power I had won but at the same time despising me as an upstart. When the Seer of Oxford named him Prince in Waiting, my father had been a common Sergeant, not yet ennobled.

But my anticipation went much amiss. His name was Eric and in character he gave the lie to his townsmen's reputation. He was olive-skinned, handsome apart from a broken nose and the scar of a sword slash on the side of his neck, and he smiled easily. He talked easily too, in the drawling accent of his city.

I could see that he was setting himself out to please me, and at first my wariness was reinforced by this. But I found there was more to him than charm: much more. When we sat alone together in my parlor, he talked good sense and with frankness.

He said: "You will know why I have come, Luke. Your reputation has traveled far, and grown as it traveled. Old stories are recalled. Of a Seance, for instance, where you were named as one who would be Prince of Princes. Men fear you for what you have achieved, and might yet achieve."

I watched him, making no comment on this. He said:

"I came expecting to find someone crazed with power and vainglory, to hunt out his weaknesses against a future conflict. I find you a reasonable man. I think our minds may not lie far apart. We are both young. We both look for change from old and stupid ways."

He smiled. "It is far worse, I think, in Oxford than in Winchester. Nothing can be done there that was not done last year. My father is not a bad man, but stern and inflexible. As a child I earned a few thrashings for not obeying the rules. After I learned to give them lip service, and keep my own counsel.

"But it is time there was change. As I say, the stories of Luke of Winchester run fast, in and out of many cities, and reach us, too. Stories of your journey to the north, where you killed the Bayemot, and stories of your conquests. But there is one I have only heard since I came here: of how you decreed a dwarf should be a warrior. I like that one. It gives a different ring to all the others."

I did not disappoint him by telling him I had done it to keep a pledge rather than to bring about change for its own sake. And though I believed him honest I could not tell him the secrets of the Seers. But here was someone who might be a strong ally when the time was ripe. He himself put it into words:

"I have fought with our army and will again if there is need. But these battles achieve nothing, serve no useful purpose. The time for petty rulers is over. We need a single government to give laws throughout the land. I think I have fathomed your aim, and if I have I agree with it. I can do nothing while my father lives, but he is an old man and sick. When I can help, I will."

I said: "I believe you, Eric. And this is good to hear."

"One other thing. You will not find me

jealous of your glory. I seek only to be your lieutenant. When the time comes I will gladly bend a knee to the Prince of Princes."

It was not in my nature to trust any but a well-tried friend, and I have learned enough of the princely craft, and of the lies and intrigues that surround it, not to be deceived by fair words and smiles. I would not relax my guard with Eric of Oxford, as my father so fatally had done with Fat Jeremy. But though I would keep my precautions I did believe him honest. And liked him also.

It would serve all my ends to bind him closer to us. As it happened, there was something which could help bring that about. He met my Captains and their Ladies, among them Edmund's sister, Jenny. And it was plain that he was taken with her.

Thereafter I took care that they were thrown together. He was, I knew, unmarried and unbetrothed, as she was. He was happy to be in Winchester, free of the gloom and protocol of Oxford. In this mood he might be glad to take a girl of this city back with him as a bride. And it would suit me very well to have him do so.

Nor was Jenny a person to whom even the Prince of Oxford could object as a future lady for his son. She came of a family that had been noble for generations—since the Disaster

—and her father had been Prince of Winchester. It would be a good match.

I told only Blodwen of my hopes. She did not dispute the advantages, but said:

"I think you will find him eager enough. I am not so sure of her."

"But she likes him. Anyone can see she does. Did you not see them laughing together only this morning?"

Blodwen smiled. "Liking is not loving."

"His looks are good enough. He is a tried warrior. He is cheerful and has a nimble wit. And he is a Prince's son, Prince in Waiting to a great city. What more could she want?"

"Poor Luke! You know how to wage war or make a treaty, but in the trivial small maze of a woman's mind you are lost utterly. Jenny does not need telling any of that; she sees it before you do. But if she does not have a heart to give, it is no help."

"But she is not betrothed!"

"No," Blodwen said, "she is not betrothed." She sighed. "I will not argue with you. Perhaps it will fall out as you hope. Luke, I must go. There is a last fitting for my gown for tonight. I do not want to disgrace you at the ball."

I was with Jenny when Blodwen came into the Hall of Mirrors. There was a sudden hush in the talk. I recalled a similar silence falling on the Wilsh court in Cymru's throne room, the night I saw her first, and turned to look.

She had brought her other dresses with her, but this one had been made by our Winchester tailors. The cloth was silk, less fine and less brightly dyed than that of the Wilsh: a dull crimson. But to make up for it they had put heavy gold braid at the neck and hem and on the deep cuffs. And they had cut it cunningly so that it clung close to her, and yet swirled from her as she walked.

I said, involuntarily: "By the Great, have you ever seen anything so lovely?"

"No," Jenny said. Her voice was small. "Never."

"I must go to her," I said. "And I think Eric is looking for you, Jenny."

"Then I suppose I must wait here until he finds me."

She turned away, and I went to Blodwen. I was almost afraid to touch her when we stood up together for the first dance, but she took my hand firmly with her small warm one, and tugged me sharply into line when I made a false step. I had never had much skill in these enterprises.

Apart from that, things went well. I saw Eric dancing with Jenny, and that pleased me.

Later I saw him go out with her through the open doors into the garden, which pleased me still more. Then, just before supper, I saw Eric on his own.

I said: "Are you looking for Jenny? I think I saw her . . ."

He cut across my words, an unusual impoliteness.

"No." He looked unhappy. "I'm sorry, Luke." He put on a smile but it was more rueful than cheerful. "I have suffered a reverse."

"A reverse? How?"

He told me. He had proposed marriage to her and been refused. And it was clear, though he did not charge her with it, that the refusal had been brusque rather than gentle.

My anger rose. I knew that hardness of Jenny's. In the past I had suffered from it. She had the right to take her own decisions, but no right to be rude to a friend of mine, a Prince I looked to as an ally.

I made excuses and left him. I looked for Jenny and soon found her. I said:

"A private word with you."

She smiled but her lips were tight. "As you wish, sire."

The garden was the nearest place. There was an arbor beyond the sundial and we had it to ourselves. We could hear the minstrels' music and see figures moving in the Hall of Mirrors, but at this spot it was quiet and private.

Jenny said: "This is the second time I have been brought here tonight."

Her voice was provocative and defiant. My anger increased. I told her what I thought of her conduct. Eric was a good man. He did not deserve to be treated with contempt.

"And did he say I did so treat him?"

"No. But he was hurt. If a woman must refuse a man she can do it decently, without wounding him."

She was silent; then said: "I did not mean to hurt him. I agree, he is a good man. But he took me by surprise, and I am not . . . accustomed to such things." I saw her look at me in the dark. "If you think it right, Luke, I will tell him I am sorry."

She had accepted the rebuke and was trying to make amends. In a calmer mood I would have realized this, and let it go. But my anger was not only on Eric's behalf. It stemmed also from the frustration of my plans. I said savagely:

"You are a fool, as well. You will get no better offer than this, nor one a tenth as good."

She stared at me. Fire came back into her voice too. She said:

"A Prince may command his people. But by what right does he tell them how to live their lives?"

"For your own good! Because you are blind, girl, to your own interest."

"Blind?" She laughed. "As blind as the Prince of Winchester?"

We faced each other in bitterness and rage. I saw the rapid rise and fall of her breast and my own pulse was racing. In the distance there was the soft murmur of voices, above the music of a minuet. I said:

"I have eyes that can tell a fool, and a friend."

"Have you? And a betrothed bride who dallies with a friend? Can they tell that?"

I laughed now. "You are not just a fool, but mad."

Her voice dropped but was burning still. "Yours are the only eyes that do not see it."

I took her arm roughly, my fingers bruising the flesh. She winced and I said:

"You tell this lie of Blodwen. I could have you whipped for that and may do yet, noble though you are. But what man do you traduce? What friend do you call false?"

"You know it. You do not need telling."

It was true. In such a catalogue of lies there could only be one name. I said:

"Edmund?"

She stared in silence and the silence gave assent. I let go her arm.

"So you charge your own brother with this. You disgust me. Without a single jot of evidence."

My contempt provoked her again.

"Listen," she said, "listen, blind Luke. Do you remember a day when we picnicked in the water meadows, and you were called away to Romsey? Edmund took her back in your place. Not to the city only but to her apartments. And stayed there after."

"At my bidding. I told Blodwen to give him his supper, in return for the rowing."

Jenny said: "They dined late that night. I went to his room after eleven, and he was not there."

"You speak out of narrowness and ignorance. The Wilsh love talking late into the night. In Klan Gothlen Edmund and I have sat with Cymru till two in the morning. Eleven is late by our standards but not by theirs."

She said nothing. In the distance the music stopped and the chatter of voices swelled up. I said:

"Exile would be better than whipping. I would rather not see your face again. But to take any action would injure Edmund. So go your way, Jenny, and keep out of mine."

She went without speaking by the path that would take her from the palace. I walked, willing myself to calmness, back to the Hall of Mirrors. Another dance had struck up as I got there. Edmund stood opposite Blodwen. They saw me look at them, and smiled.

A troop of players came to us that winter. They were not the ordinary strolling players, who acted their parts in any room large enough, or in the open air, and sent one of their numbers round with a greasy cap to collect money off their audience. These were more ambitious. In Salisbury they had had what they called a theater, and they took a disused malt-house to make a similar place in our city. It was in the River Road, not far from my Aunt Mary's house.

This was one more sign of how Winchester's importance was growing in men's eyes. Players, like thieves and tricksters, will always flock where there are full pockets to be emptied, and they had heard talk of our wealth and prosperity. But it was not just a question of money. Their chief player and manager, a lean arrogant man in his thirties with a black

pointed beard and showy dress, let it be
known that they had come because it was fitting that the greatest city should have the
greatest company of players.

This swaggering was typical of him. When
he paid his respects to me and to my Captains,
he brought his hat down in a bow that caused
the feather on top of it to sweep the floor, but
the gesture was empty. He made it plain that
in truth he thought little of warriors or nobles, or anyone who did not belong to his own
seedy profession. And that in that profession
he believed that no other could come near
him. I had never met even a Prince with such
overweening pride.

Of my own inclination I would have sent
him packing back to Salisbury. But his reputation had traveled ahead of him. The people
were anxious to see these players, and it was
true that if they were any good they would
help relieve the winter's tedium. Blodwen
spoke for them also. She had been used to
plays and theaters in her own city, and missed
these diversions.

So they set to work to turn the malt-house
to their ends, and dwarfs worked busily under
the direction of this man who called himself,
in further illustration of his modesty, the
Player King. At last it was finished, and news
of the first play cried in the streets. His mes-

senger came to the palace, humbly inviting me and my court to be present at the opening.

We arrived as a gray evening was turning into a hard black night. Snow which had threatened all day had not yet come, but the frost was sharp. A knifing wind blew from the east.

Inside braziers had been set up and it was less cold, but we still had need of our cloaks. The dwarfs had done their work well, and I acknowledged that the direction had been good. The walls had been brightly painted, and the ceiling also. And the floor had been constructed to be on three levels. The highest part was at the back where there were benches for the common people, but empty now. Then came the section where chairs were set out for us. Below that again was the part they called the stage. A heavy curtain, draped from ceiling to floor, covered the front of it.

When we were seated the Player King came. He said to me:

"Are you comfortable, sire?"

There was that in his voice which suggested that our discomfort would insult him. I said:

"Well enough. And it is a fine theater. Though some might think it strange that you set the commons above their betters."

He smiled. "Would you rather they came between you and the stage? As it is, if they were not raised up they would see little of the play. And you must remember, sire, that in the realm of dream and imagination all men are equal." He bowed. "It is our privilege to offer a place in which even a Prince can put aside both cares and crown for an hour in exchange for the airy stuff of fantasy."

He said it glibly. What was not said because no saying was needed was that not all in fact were equal here: others must yield to the authority of the Player King. I said shortly:

"What play will you give us?"

"It is called 'Tristram and Iseult,'" he said. "I have written it myself, though the story is ancient." He bowed again. "And if you are ready, sire, we will waste no further time."

He pulled his cloak about him and went through the curtains onto the stage. Soon after that the curtains drew away to either side. Some of the ladies exclaimed with pleasure. In front of us was the representation of a throne room. There were two thrones, painted to look like gold, and other gaudy trappings. Although the space was small, the eye was deceived into seeing grandeur there. Side walls had pillars cunningly painted on them, and at the back a painted window looked out and down to crags in a bright blue sea. It was the palace of a great king, set high on a sea-girt cliff. And into the throne room from a door at one side, his cloak thrown off to show a dress of garish magnificence and a golden crown on his head, strode the Player King.

He played the part of Mark, king of this imaginary country. The story told how Mark had a lieutenant and friend called Tristram, whom he sent on his behalf to request the hand of the daughter of the king in a land called Ire. The contract was made and Tristram brought Iseult, the daughter, back with him to Mark's court.

Iseult's mother, seeking to ensure her daughter's happiness, gave a love potion to the serving maid who was to go with her. This was to be given to Mark before the wedding, and would ensure that he loved her all his days. But Tristram and Iseult, not knowing what it was, found the flask with the potion and drank it together. So they must love each other, as long as they should live.

A strange uneasiness grew in me as this tale unfolded. I had expected to be bored, never having had much taste for minstrels or mummers but this was not boredom. I felt a sickness in my stomach, a tightness in my chest as though a giant's hand gripped my heart.

A scene came in which, with long poetic speeches, Tristram and Iseult declared their love but swore to fight against it. Tristram was Mark's friend, Iseult his affianced bride. They knew they loved each other but they would not betray him. And as they talked on the stage they drew closer together and then, still swearing they would never yield to love, embraced and kissed.

It was a moment of high drama. All eyes, it seemed, were fixed upon the players. But my eyes went to Blodwen. I saw her look not at the stage but at Edmund; and as though word had gone silently from heart to heart his eyes met hers. For a long moment they locked, then turned away.

The sickness and tightness grew worse, and coldness was added to them. My legs shivered. I had to clamp my jaw tight to keep my teeth from chattering.

I had tried to put aside all thought of what Jenny had said in the garden. If by chance the memory came to me I dismissed it. Now all flooded back. I heard the soft music again in the distance and heard her voice, hard with contempt: "Listen . . . Listen, blind Luke. . ."

The play ran its course. I saw nothing in it but resemblances. Tristram was a skilled player of the harp and sang a love song to Iseult. I thought of Edmund playing his lute in the water meadows and singing: "Green-sleeves was all my joy, Greensleeves was my delight . . ." The Player King made Mark a man stupidly blind to what was happening, concerned only with the affairs of state, a dull and heavy creature. I saw myself riding away to Romsey, leaving the pleasant scene behind.

And there rage supplanted sickness. Jenny had said: "Yours are the only eyes that do not see it." Could that be true? Could the fact of my betrayal be as clear as Mark's was? Was it the talk of Winchester? The Player King had said he had written the play himself. Were these things jibes at me?

I had an urge to leap down onto the stage, to knock aside the wooden sword the Player King wore with my steel one, and spit him with it. But as always my mind worked coldly behind my rage. There might be killing needed yet, but this was not the time.

The play ended somehow. Mark killed Tristram, I think, and Iseult stabbed herself. I was only concerned that it should be over. The players paraded for our applause and then the Player King came to me again, and asked if their poor efforts had met with my approval.

"It was entertaining," I said, "as these things go."

He bowed stiffly, disconcerted. Blodwen said:

"Oh, it was good! We have no better players in Klan Gothlen. And the play was finely
written. Luke, you must reward him well."

I saw her face, candid and eager, and could
not believe her false. Behind her Edmund
smiled at me, as he had done many times, over
her enthusiasm. If they were not honest the
whole world was a stinking ruin, broken and
slimed like the village which the Bayemot
overran. And I had killed the Bayemot. I said
to the Player King:

"You played well. Gold will be sent you in
the morning."

But in the night I woke, and having wak-
ened did not sleep again. Scenes from the play
came back to me; the words of the two lovers
rang in my ears with Jenny's mocking voice
behind them. "Listen . . . Listen, blind
Luke . . ." I tossed and turned and, rising
early, took a horse and rode out of the North
Gate, past the astonished watch.

I rode hard and far, like a coward fleeing
from a battlefield. But there was no escaping
this battle; its blind and hateful warriors har-
ried me without mercy, and a hundred swords
pierced me. And I knew there was no medi-
cine to heal these wounds.

So I came back, tired and sick at heart, to

the city which I ruled. I had become a slave to my own eyes and ears. I must watch them both, listen to every word that passed between them, interpret every gesture. While I did so, I must hide my misery.

And in my slavery I was tossed to and fro. I would see her look at him, and fill with anger. Then she would look at me, wide-eyed and smiling, and the anger would turn to love, and self-disgust. I had no interest in anything else. My Captains came to me, with news or questions, and I listened and spoke and a moment later did not know what they had said or I had replied.

Days passed. I had no appetite but forced myself to eat, dully chewing and swallowing the food which like everything else but one thing had become meaningless. My life was consumed with watching, guessing. Then one night, when we had both been guests in his mother's house, he handed her her cloak on parting and I saw his hand rest, for another long moment, on her shoulder.

We walked through the streets toward the palace; for so short a distance we had not brought horses. They were less dark than they had been: last winter I had had oil lamps put up such as they had in Salisbury. Blodwen hummed a tune. I said:

"Are you happy?"

"Yes!"

"Are you thinking yet of returning to Klan Gothlen?"

She glanced at me in surprise. "Why, no."

"You have been a long time here."

She laughed. "Have I outstayed my welcome, then?"

"If you do not go soon, you will be caught by the winter."

"Would that be so terrible a thing?"

I said slowly: "I was wondering . . . what is it that keeps you."

"I have told you. I love your city. More than my own, I think."

I said: "What person?"

"What person? Who else but Luke, Prince of three cities?"

She said the words lightly, jesting, but there was a falseness. I asked:

"What of Edmund?"

"I am fond of Edmund, and all your friends."

"Only fond?"

She stopped. We stood under an oil lamp. Some distance away a polymuf, made still more crooked in shape by the shadows which surrounded him, scuttled into an alley. We were alone. Blodwen said:

"Speak openly, Luke, and honestly."

My throat swelled and I had to force words from it.

"This," I said. "Have you betrayed me with Edmund?"

Her eyes looked into mine unflinchingly. "I have not betrayed you with Edmund, or anyone."

My misery lifted. I could live again as a free man, not a fugitive from nightmares. I said:

"You swear this?"

"If swearing is needed, I swear it."

I wanted only one thing more. I took her hands.

"And you do not love him? You will swear that, too?"

She smiled, and for the instant all was well. Then she shook her head.

"No," she said softly. "That I will not swear."

5

The Council of Captains

I sent word very early to Edmund that I wished him to ride with me. It was still dark when we clattered down the High Street, drawing curses from an upper room where the noise of our passing roused some good citizen from sleep, across the river and along the road to East Gate.

He asked me when we met what reason there was for our journey, at such an hour. I told him he would know in good time. It had crossed my mind that Blodwen might have sent word to him herself, telling him of what had passed between us, and I searched his face for sign of this. But the bewilderment there was real; he truly did not know why I had come for him. He shrugged his shoulders and, accepting his Prince's command as a Captain must, mounted and rode with me.

The guard saluted us as we left the city. I set no frenzied pace as I had done on that recent solitary ride. Then my adversaries had been phantasms of the mind. Now there was only one, who had a face and rode at my side. The sky ahead was paling with the dawn. I looked behind me at the gate and remembered my father's head, stuck on a spear above it. I had thought life could bring no greater anguish than that. It seemed a small thing now.

We traveled in silence. Edmund was not unused to this. I had had my times of silence before, when my mind was busy with some project and I saw no need of speech, and he had accustomed himself to them. The city slept behind us. There was only the sound of hoofs and harness and our horses' breaths snorting in the chilly air.

We reached the Elder Pond, black and rimmed with ice, and I took the fork that led to the Contest Field. I reined my horse in when we reached it. It lay bare and empty, with the dark mass of Catherine's Hill behind it. On the hill's top its grove of trees stood like mourners against the ashen sky. I thought of this place as I had seen it once, with the sun shining after rain on a spring day, and the

whole city, it seemed, cheering the Young
Captains as they led their teams in for the
Contest.

There had been something to win then,
too, and against great odds. I remembered my
young self. Had I fought so hard for no more
than a jeweled sword?

Edmund kept the silence. I said at last:

"Do you recall the time we fought here?"

"Of course."

"And how I beat you."

He smiled. "That, too."

"You said once, when we watched another
Contest together, that on a second chance you
would have won."

"Did I, Luke?" He shook his head. "I do
not remember that."

"Do you still think so?"

"That I would have beaten you? No. I
knew that after you had killed the Bayemot. I
have some courage but when the odds are
hopeless I draw back. You would always beat
me; not so much because you are a better
fighter as because you will not accept defeat."

I paused before I said: "At least some good
came of it."

"Yes. You rule three cities, and will rule
more."

I said: "Our friendship."

"Yes. A better thing still."

"It has meant much to me. I have Captains who serve me well, a dwarf warrior who would die for me, but those things are not friendship. There were three of us: you, Martin and I. Martin turned Acolyte and now has left us altogether, to go to Sanctuary. Only you and I remain."

There was a faraway honking and high up small dots trailed across the gray. Wild geese, on their journey to lands we would never know. I said:

"Let us talk of Blodwen, Edmund."

Our eyes met. He said slowly: "What of her?"

"I think you know."

He did not deny that, but said: "There has been nothing between us."

"Nothing?" I spoke bitterly. "No looks, no touches of hands?"

"No more than that."

"Listen," I said, "she is mine. Cymru gave her to me at the banquet at which we both sat, after the killing of the Bayemot. Is this not true?"

"Yes," Edmund said. "But she is a girl, not something to be given."

In the mind's eye I saw Blodwen again, as she stood with me on the staircase above her father's throne room, and heard her voice: "I am not an honor—I am Blodwen! I will be my own woman. Remember that, Luke of Winchester." I said:

"Is it the office of a friend to come between a man and his betrothed bride, even with a single look?"

Then he looked ashamed. He said in a low voice:

"It was not meant. I promise you."

"You could not help it?"

"No."

"Perhaps you could not. I do not think I blame you. But you are a free man. You can make an end of it now."

He did not speak. I said:

"I claim this for our friendship's sake."

The wind blew cold down Catherine's Hill and our horses stamped their feet. Edmund spoke at last.

"I will end it."

I reached across and clasped his arm. "I will not forget this! And now, I have a mission for you."

He looked startled. "A mission?"

"To Oxford. To talk in public with its Prince; in private with its Prince in Waiting. I look for two alliances, one open, the other secret."

Edmund said: "How long will the mission last?"

"I will expect you back in the spring. We

will watch the Contest of the Young Captains together."

"And when would you have me go?"

"Today."

"Be open with me," he said. "It is because of Blodwen that I am to be sent away? Such a mission would be better in older hands than mine."

"You have been too free with her. This you admit. You said you could not help it and I believe you. All things wither without nourishment. It is better that you do not see her for a time."

I twitched my horse's rein, turning her head back toward the city. Edmund said: "Hold, Luke."

"Well?"

"Have you spoken to Blodwen of this?"

It might have been better to lie, but I could not.

"Yes."

"What did you say to her?"

"I asked her if she had betrayed me with you. She swore she had not. I knew she spoke truth."

"And what else?"

I echoed him: "What else?"

His voice had changed. There was boldness in it.

"You put a question to her and got your

answer. But still you need to send me away to Oxford. Is it only my weakness you fear? What reassurance did you seek from Blodwen, and not find?"

I said: "What passes between Blodwen and me is our concern, not yours."

"You are wrong, Luke! I will not go on your mission until I have put a question to her. And if her answer is what I think it may be then you must find another man for Oxford."

I felt cold again: a cold sharper and more inward than that which the wind scoured from the ugly sky.

"You will not try to take her from me."

"Not unless she puts out a hand to me. But if she does, nothing will stop me taking it."

"Not friendship?"

"Not anything!"

He spoke exultantly. I said:

"And if I beg you?"

All my body trembled. I felt tears start in my eyes, and blinked them back.

He said: "Do not beg for something which I cannot give."

"Cannot, or will not?"

"What difference is there? There are strengths beyond our own."

I said, wonderingly, to myself almost: "I never doubted your loyalty. I would have doubted my own sooner. I know my weaknesses and I gave you best in friendship. But I could not do such injury to a friend. I would die first."

The day was lighter, and I saw him flush. He said:

"You are my friend, but Blodwen I love. There is a difference in our natures. I do not think you have ever truly loved. Or ever could."

"I loved you," I said, "who were my friend."

He shook his head. "Talking does no good."

"Listen," I said. "Forget friendship, if it means so little to you. Have you thought of the harm that can come from this? Not just to us, but to the city."

"You have got your city," he said. "Keep it. We do not want it."

He linked her desires with his, as though of right. Pain raked its claws through me. I said:

"Even if I would, I could not let you have her. I am Prince of the city and she, daughter of the King of the Wilsh, is to be my bride. If it is not held to I am no Prince, and chaos follows."

"Then let it follow. You cannot stop us, Luke."

"I am Prince," I said. "I have some powers."

We rode together back to the city and in

silence. The guard saluted us again at the East Gate, and I bade him bring the Sergeant. He was out of the guardhouse on the instant. His name was Tunney, one of Harding's men, old for a warrior but still powerful. I pointed to Edmund.

"Arrest him."

Blodwen said: "Luke, what have you done?"

Her face was white and she showed signs of haste. She had come unannounced to where I sat in my parlor. It was early still. Outside the window a few small flakes of snow drifted slowly down.

I said: "In what way, lady?"

"They say that Edmund is under guard. Because of what I said last night? I promise you . . ."

I thought she might lie, to save him, and did not want to hear it. I cut across her words.

"I gave an order to a Captain and he refused to obey it. That is all and that is enough."

"What order?"

I told her of the mission to Oxford. Her eyes were on my face as I spoke, and I watched her watching me. At the end she said only:

"What will you do to him?"

"A Prince must have obedience from his Captains, in peace as much as in war. You know this. Disobedience imperils the city and merits death. But I will do him no harm. I will only banish him."

"You cannot do it, Luke."

"I must," I said, "or see a man walking the streets of Winchester who had defied my authority. Would you rather I kept him in perpetual imprisonment? Even that would be too great a risk to take."

"The order should not have been given," she said. "It was not done for the city but for your private ends."

I shook my head. "There is no difference."

"You believe that?"

"A Prince must, or he is no Prince."

I put strength into my voice to answer her, but at heart I felt weary, and a dull sickness racked me.

Blodwen said: "What am I in this? A thing? A creature to do her master's bidding, and get a smile from him and perhaps a bauble or two in reward? Are we all *things* to the Prince of Winchester?"

"I do what has to be done."

"And must we dance to the tune you think you hear? Last night you asked me to swear I did not love Edmund, and I would not do it. Because of that you ordered him on this mission. Did you trust me so little?"

I made no answer. She said:

"We are not puppets, though you would have us so. I do not know what would have happened if you had left well alone. It is no news to me that Edmund loves me, and no surprise that he will defy his Prince for my sake. But I have known his mind better than I knew my own. I would not swear it, not because it was untrue but because I did not know if it were true or not. My father proclaimed our betrothal and I would not willingly thwart his wishes. But I tell you this, Luke: if Edmund is banished then I will go with him and share his exile."

Her words lashed me, with fear as well as pain. In combat I had never known such terror. I looked at her face, unsmiling, lacking any gentleness. I wanted to admit defeat and in doing so beg mercy. I might have still won her if I had. Compassion might not show in her face but it was in her heart always. In defeat I might have conquered.

But I could not trap her with her own pity. I said:

"You may not do it, lady. I am still Prince here, and forbid it."

She smiled then, but with no softening.

"I am not your subject, Luke of Winchester."

"You are in my city."

"My father is Cymru, King of the Wilsh. If

I do his bidding it is with consent. No other ruler can bind me."

I felt the fear again, the weakness that was a worse pain than pain. By fighting I must lose everything in the world worth having, and gain nothing. But I could not go back. We faced each other across the narrow room. Behind Blodwen hung the picture of my mother. There, too, was beauty; a beauty which I had worshiped but which had given me small comfort.

I raised my voice: "Guard!"

He clomped in from his post in the Hall of Mirrors. Blodwen still stared at me. I said to the guard:

"The Lady Blodwen is under arrest."

He said impassively: "Yes, sire."

Blodwen said: "Will you throw me in your dungeon?"

Her voice was angry and incredulous. I said:

"Conduct her to her apartments. See that she is well guarded there."

Grimm, the Seer, came to me in mid-morning. He looked as large and easy of mind as ever, but he said:

"Things are in a sorry mess, Luke."

I said: "I have known them better."

"All was going so well." He shook his head.

"We must not have an injury to our plans at this stage."

He meant the plans of the High Seers: the plans to restore Science and machines, to transform men's lives. Children's voices called outside as they played some game. The hopes and schemes of the Seers mattered as little to me.

"What do you plan to do with them?" Grimm asked. I did not answer. "Will you hear my advice?"

I said, listening to my own voice's echo and amazed by its seeming calm:

"I will always hear your advice, Grimm."

"Send her back at once to her father's court."

"She will not go without Edmund."

"Then send him with her. Klan Gothlen is far enough away. It is no threat to us."

"And he will have her."

The calmness must have wavered. Grimm stretched his bulky body in the chair. He said:

"Before I became an Acolyte there was a girl from whom I got much misery. Some of our order find it hard to be deprived of women in their lives. I have been glad of it. There are other pleasures."

His belly proved his point. I said:

"I am glad, for your sake."

"Her name was Lucy," Grimm said. "The

hurt at the time was great: I thought I would have died of it. But I did not, as you see. And though I remember her name I cannot recall her face. All things pass."

He waited but I said nothing. He said:

"Be careful, Luke. Do nothing rash. Much hangs on you."

I had another visitor: the Christian Bishop. When his name was brought to me, as one requesting audience, I thought of saying no. But any company was better than the company of my thoughts. So I let him in, and looked at him indifferently.

"What do you want?" I asked. "More of my bounty? Have you not had gold and land enough?"

He said: "Men gather in the streets. Only a few so far but the numbers may grow. They cry a name, Prince, but it is not yours. They cry 'Blodwen.' She is well loved by your people."

I laughed. "I have had the Seers telling me what to do but I did not think the Christians would send their Bishop! I did not know you took such interest in the affairs of state."

"Nor do we. I do not speak of politics but of people. One person in particular. She is a good woman."

I stared at him, half angry, half amused.

"That is true, Bishop."

"And honest."

"True also."

"She has done you no wrong." I said nothing to that. "And if you wrong her you will wrong yourself far more."

"I am a Prince," I said. "Remember it."

He shrugged his heavy shoulders and his bald head bobbed.

"That is what they call you. But you are a man first, and she a woman."

"What do you know of men and women? Are you not celibate, to please your god?"

"I know this," he said. "I know that what moves you is not love but pride."

"Of course," I said, "your god called pride a sin. And you cannot be expected to know better. You are not a warrior."

"Whether it be sin or not," he said, "your pride could yet destroy you. Not all your warriors nor your own right arm will save you then."

"You weary me, Bishop," I said. "Go back and pray to your god who had no pride."

Lastly Jenny came. She had been weeping and her eyes were still red. I said:

"Lady, what service would you do me now?"

"Only to right a wrong."

"No wrong. You called me blind and that

was true. My eyes are opened and I thank you."

"There was no truth in it! Edmund did not betray you. I lied in anger." She looked at me, her face a mask of shame. "And in jealousy. I could not bear the way you looked at her. Forgive me, Luke. And do not hold my lies against Edmund." She drew sobbing breath. "Nor against her."

If I had pity to spare I would have pitied her. All that she said was true, and made no difference. I said wearily:

"They love each other. What comes of this must come. There is no profit in regrets."

She turned from me, weeping again, and went away.

I heard the tumult and ran out, my sword bare. The noise came from the north wing, where Blodwen's apartments were. When I got there I found frightened polymufs, splintered doors, one guard dying and one dead. The dying man could not speak and the polymufs were too incoherent to make much sense. There had been fighting, they said, which was plain enough. It was plain also that they had seen nothing because they had hidden out of the way.

But the door to Blodwen's room was smashed, and she was gone.

I was still standing there five minutes later,

staring at the broken door, when Greene rode down Sack Street with a dozen of his troop. He dismounted. There was blood on his sleeve but he did not seem badly hurt. I roused myself and said:

"Who took her?"

"Charles."

"*Charles?* How? By himself?"

Because he was Edmund's brother I had that morning, as a precaution, split his troop among other Captains.

Greene said: "He picked up half a dozen of his men. They surprised the guard here. We gave chase but . . ."

"You lost them? It makes no difference. Half a dozen men? He must be mad. And what good does it do to take her? Does he think to use her as a bargain for Edmund's release?"

"He has released Edmund already." I stared at him. "They have the citadel. That was what turned us back."

"Then Blaine . . ." Blaine's men had taken over the citadel guard that morning. "Blaine is with him in this."

Greene nodded. "It seems so."

"So it is rebellion. And Blaine thinks that with his troop and what he can bring together of Charles's, he can take this city?"

"There is more. He has given the Wilsh

their swords back. I saw them on the citadel wall."

Disarming Blodwen's Wilsh bodyguard had been another precaution. It was hard to believe that even Blaine could do such a thing as to arm foreign soldiers within the city. But I had no time to waste on incredulity. The revolt was a major one and must be put down. I said to Greene:

"He will be looking for others who may go over to him if they think he is strong enough to win. We need to establish our own strength fast. We must rally those captains on whom we can rely and get them together, Wilson and Ripon, Nicoll, Barnes, Becket, Stuart."

Greene nodded.

I said: "You go for Nicoll and Barnes. I will get the others. We assemble here, in the palace yard."

By dusk the lines were drawn. I had failed with Stuart, who had taken his men over to Blaine, and Turner's troop was also in the citadel; but I had expected that. Grant, about whom I had been unsure, on the other hand had stayed loyal. We held the palace and the city in general, they the citadel.

Much hinged on what Harding might do. His troop was perhaps the strongest of all. If they joined us we must win easily: the citadel

offered a strong defense but it had never been
meant to be impregnable. The city's walls and
its warriors had always been our chief safe-
guard. If he went over to Blaine I was still
confident of the outcome, though the fighting
would be harder and bloodier.

Harding was no fool; he knew this also.
And though he had been no friend of my father or my brother, and was no friend of
mine, the hatred between his family and
Blaine's went back much further. Nor could I
see him joining a rebel who had put arms into
the hands of barbarians. He might be treach-
erous but he loved the city.

The fact that he had not committed himself
so far, but kept his troop at that great house
of his which was not much smaller than the
palace, meant only, I guess, that he relished
the importance of his position. All must see
that we waited for him. But he would not put
things off too long in case, from impatience, I
attacked without him. We could win without
his help and that would make him as little as
the other made him great.

He came in fact at the hour I expected, and
was shown into the hall where I sat with the
loyal Captains. He greeted me as a Captain
should greet his Prince, the bow brief but un-
stinted. I said:

"Welcome, Captain! We are glad to have

you at our conference. Your counsel will serve us well."

He said: "This is a bad business, sire."

"It is but can soon be ended."

"Soon maybe, but bitterly. The hatred will not die when the heads of five Captains of Winchester are spiked above the palace gate. The feuds which start today will last for generations."

I said: "This may be so. But we did not start them. What would you have me do?"

"It is said that you were to pronounce banishment on Edmund."

"He refused a command I gave him. Do I not have the right?"

Harding nodded. "You have it. And banishment is better than bloodshed. It might serve better for others, also."

"I am willing to give them exile instead of death. You can take that message to them, if you wish."

"There is a better way. If such a message is sent all must accept or all refuse. They will refuse it therefore. But if we call them to a Captains' conclave, under flag of truce, there is a chance to win them over one by one."

He spoke persuasively, and I saw one or two of our company nod their heads. They were loyal but none was eager for the slaughter of old comrades, in many cases kinfolk. I was not eager for it myself. If it could be settled without bloodshed so much the better. And even if Charles and Edmund and Blaine proved obdurate, Turner and Stuart might not.

I said: "Will they come to such a conclave at the palace, do you think? I will not go to them."

Harding said: "There is my house. It lies between."

We sat in the great hall of Harding's house, at his council table. It was more magnificent than anything I had in the palace: very long, oval in shape, made of oak that generations of polymuf servants had polished to a dark bloom.

I was at the head, with Greene on my right and the other loyal Captains near. Blaine and his rebels, including Edmund, took the other end of the table. Harding sat in the space between.

We had our swords but were bound in honor not to use them. I did not fear treachery. In any case we outnumbered them and had men within call.

I spoke first and briefly. They were in rebellion against their Prince. It was an act which by law and ancient custom deserved death. This must follow once we had crushed them, and our power to do so was plain.

I offered them their lives, not from weakness but from desire to avoid the spilling of blood. If they surrendered, their men would suffer no penalty. They themselves could take with them into exile whatever movable goods they wished.

Blaine answered me. In Winchester men accepted the rule of Princes but not of tyrants. A Prince might command anything of his Captains but only while his commands served the general welfare. It had not been so in this case. A form of exile had been trumped up against one who had done no wrong, and when it had rightly been rejected banishment had been pronounced. This was tyranny, and it was the duty of citizens to oppose it.

He spoke with his usual bluster. We were all accustomed to it and I did not think anyone was much impressed. In the light of the oil lamps that hung from the ceiling I thought I saw unease in the small eyes, deep set in the fat face.

They would make an offer, he said, in answer to mine. They did not seek bloodshed, either, but peace. If I rescinded the edict of banishment on Edmund and the order of arrest on the lady Blodwen, and restored

Charles's troop to him, and promised full amnesty to all, they would come out of the citadel and return to their homes.

It was absurd, of course. After such a confrontation as this there could be no trust. There would be two armies prowling the city, armed and ready to fight at the first provocation. Nor would it be long in coming. And having given way, what authority could I command then? I gave him a blunt refusal, without argument or explanation.

Other Captains spoke. They spoke in accordance with their places at the table, and their temperaments. Some blew hotter and some colder, but the deadlock did not break. Then, when all had had their way, Harding rose to his feet.

I had been waiting for this. His family's nobility was as ancient as Blaine's. He himself had not only served the city well but, unlike fat Blaine, had a reputation for wisdom and sound thinking. When my father was killed it had been Harding who had rallied the Captains. If Peter had not retaken the city there was little doubt he would have been proclaimed Prince. His voice on our side counted for more than all the others put together.

And there was something else. I had spoken to him privately on the way here. Edmund and Charles must go, and Blaine with them, but I had told him that if he asked for pardon for Stuart and Turner I would grant it. They could keep their troops, and even their places in my council. If he put it to them as a duty to the city I was sure they would accept. In this way we would split Blaine's forces; and he himself, seeing his situation as hopeless, would probably choose banishment rather than certain death. Harding had listened to me, and nodded.

Now he spoke quietly. He spoke of the city, and of the men who had served it through many generations. He did not pick out the deeds of his own family: he did not need to. He spoke of old battles. Victories had united the men of Winchester, but defeats scarcely less. Triumph and disaster had been met together, enjoyed or endured together.

He had their ear. I watched Stuart and Turner, and saw how they were affected. He was leading them with cunning. They would be his men even before he asked for their pardon and I granted it.

But he was in no hurry. He spoke of the increase, in recent years, in the city's power and prosperity. This had happened under the rule of the Perrys. Although not of ancient nobility this family had served the city well: Prince Luke—he bowed slightly to me—not least. When one thought of the city, of its great past and greater future, what did it matter where a girl, even the daughter of a king, bestowed her affections? The Wilsh were a faraway people, and no concern of ours.

I saw Stuart thump the table, and thought: we have them!

Harding paused before he spoke again. He said:

"That is the credit balance. There are also debits to consider. Power and prosperity have grown, but so have discord and intrigue. There has been treachery and plotting and murder, more than was ever known before. And so we come to this moment, with the Captains in arms against each other, the city divided.

"I have said that the affections of a girl do not matter, and that is true. But it involves the Prince, and the Prince involves us all. Can the Prince pardon those who, for any reason, have taken sword against him? And if he does, will not the city fall into new dissension, having a Prince whom none respect?"

He paused once more. "Luke, as Prince, has brought honor to our city. He is a great warrior, though young, and rules not only here but in Petersfield and Romsey as well. But being young he has made mistakes. He burned wheatfields in front of Petersfield, a thing utterly condemned by the Spirits. He made a dwarf warrior, contrary to all custom. And now he has, through passion, brought us to the verge of civil war."

Anger rose in me. There was no mistaking the change in tone. I knew myself betrayed again and got to my feet. With my hand on my sword hilt, I said:

"Do you challenge me, then, Harding? Does any man?"

Harding shook his head. "I do not challenge you, Luke. There has been enough challenging, enough making and unmaking of Princes. I ask you to do this city a greater service than you have so far done. I ask you to abdicate from ruling."

I laughed. "So that you may peacefully take my place?"

"No." He looked not at me but along the table at the Captains. "Times change. The office of Prince was once a necessary thing, binding the citizens together. But the city has grown and will grow, and it unites us no longer. We are the city, gentlemen, we few. It is we who have the power to rule it, and the responsibility to exercise that power. Today has shown something: that what divides us divides the city. We no longer need one man to tell us what to do. Our wisdom joined together is greater than that of any Prince.

"If one of us challenged Luke and took his

place, what good would that do? Would the intrigue and dissension cease? I think they might grow worse. But if power is shared between us there can be an end to envy. What do you think of this?"

The shout of approval from Blaine's end of the table was only to be expected. But I heard others shout with them: Nicoll and Ripon, Becket and Grant and Barnes.

Harding waited until they were quiet, then he said:

"I ask you again, Luke, to do this service. Abdicate peacefully. Join us as a free and equal Captain. You will be welcome in our council."

Their faces swam before me; I was half blind with rage. I said:

"You know your answer."

"Then I must put another proposition to the assembly," Harding said. "That we dismiss this Prince, doing him no hurt, and exile him from our city. Raise your right hands, all who approve of it."

Their hands went up: Blaine's, Edmund's, Charles's, Stuart's and Turner's. And with them Nicoll's, Ripon's, Becket's, Grant's, Barnes's. At last, slowly, without looking at me, Greene raised his hand with the rest. Only old Wilson sat unmoving.

"The majority favors it," Harding said.

"We rest the authority of Winchester in the council of Captains."

I said: "I claim the right of any Prince to challenge his usurper! Or will you make an end of honor?"

"There is no usurper, Captain Perry," Harding said. "And the word Prince has lost its meaning. Leave us, and go in peace into your exile."

I half-drew my sword. Their eyes watched me, my enemies and my false friends. There were enough who would be glad of the excuse to cut me down. I let the sword slip back.

"This is not the end," I said. "I am your Prince still, and the day will come when you know it. Remember today's work well. There will be a bloody harvest from this sowing."

Harding smiled. "Go in peace, while you still may."

I turned and left them.

6

A Weapon from the Past

I saw another dawn break next day, for I left the city while it was still dark. I would not stay for daylight and accept the shame of pointing fingers and the jeers of the mob. And revenge spurred me on equally with shame. The sooner I was away, the sooner I could return. Harding's head, I vowed, would sit above those of the rest.

While I was in the stables, saddling my horse, I heard a sound from the shadows behind me. I turned swiftly, hand on sword. It was not impossible, not even unlikely, that for all the talk of doing me no hurt, an assassin or more than one had been put to seek me out and kill me. Both Blaine and Harding were capable of it.

But the figure spoke as it came forward. "It

is I, sire." I recognized the dwarfish frame. It was Hans.

I said: "How did you know I would be here?"

"I did not," Hans said, "but I knew you would need your horse. I was waiting until you came."

"All night?"

He shrugged. "I dozed. We dwarfs are easy sleepers."

I took his hand. "It was a kind thought, to bid me good-by. I am glad of it."

"Not that, sire. I came to travel with you."

"No. That too warms me. But the journey I go I must make alone. Return to your home, Hans."

He said quietly, in his deep rasping voice:

"I have no home here now."

I recalled what he had said a moment before: "we dwarfs." He had left Dwarftown to serve me as a warrior. That was something which could not survive my going. He had lost everything as I had done, and it mattered as much to him as it did to me.

"Then come with me," I said. I laughed. "The High Seers must take us both together."

"The High Seers?" He was startled. "You go to Sanctuary, sire?"

Dwarfs did not pay much attention to the Spirits, but it was a dread thought to envisage

going to the place men said was their strong-
hold. I said:

"You need not go there if you fear it. We
will find a place where you can wait for me.
In Salisbury, perhaps."

"I will go where you go, sire. I do not fear
it."

"Good!" I said. "But no 'sires,' Hans. 'Sire'
is for Princes and I am Prince no longer. You
may call me Captain: they have left me that."

Hans shook his head. "You are Prince to
me, sire. And always will be."

It was strange that the loyalty of a single
man, a dwarf, could mean more than a city's
acclamation. I turned my face away.

"Saddle yourself a horse, Hans," I said.
"Take which you will. All are sound beasts.
This was the Prince's stable."

We spent that night at the court of Prince
Matthew of Andover.

The last time I had been his guest had been
on my journey south with Ezzard, after Peter
called me back from Sanctuary. But we had
met more recently, when he came to Winchester for the ball in Blodwen's honor. I had
had much flattery from him then.

He was a stupid amiable man, with a thin
dull face and scanty reddish hair. His chief
concern, as far as one could see, was cere-

mony. The army of Andover might not do conspicuously well in battle, but no other city's troops could match them in turnout and parade drill. The guard that saluted us at the gate wore a breastplate that he must have sat up all night polishing.

The pigeons, I knew, would have brought news of what had happened in Winchester. People gathered in small knots as we rode through the streets, silent and curious. At the palace—not a large building but freshly painted in stripes of black and white—we dismounted and I left Hans with the horses. I was admitted to Matthew's council chamber, and he wasted no time in making the position clear.

He remained seated as I crossed the room toward him. I bowed and said:

"Greetings, sire."

He did not return the bow. With a stiff face, he said:

"Greetings, Captain Perry."

But once he had established what we two were—himself a Prince and I a landless wanderer—he could permit some amiability to show again. He ordered a room to be prepared for me in the palace and bade me join him that evening at his table. And I mustered the grace somehow to thank him for his hospitality.

I told myself that I could spurn no possible ally, even this fool with his passion for putting things neatly in rows. At supper that night I talked of what had happened. This embarrassed him but he offered cold sympathy. I led him to the point I wished to make, putting it broadly enough to penetrate his narrow skull but delicately as befitted one who was no longer a royal cousin but a vagabond. The point was this: if one city could unmake its Prince and replace him by a council of Captains, others might do likewise.

He took it but was not impressed. From stupidity again, I thought, and lack of imagination, but I misjudged him there. He said, with more cunning than I would have given him credit for:

"Who proposed your deposition in that council? Harding. So at the outset he speaks for the others. It is a council of Captains but one man is its voice. How long before he has a Prince's power, and once he has that will he not take the name?"

It was something that had occurred to me also. Blaine would fight him to the end, but Blaine was no match for him in craft. Nor would Blaine's arming of the Wilsh be soon forgotten.

I said: "This may be. But if such a pretext can be used once it can be used again. It sets the authority of Captains above that of Prince."

"I do not think so, Perry." My own name was an insult. He smiled complacently. "I am safe from challenge from my Captains."

"As short a time since as yesterday morning, I thought the same."

Impatience and anger had sharpened my voice. He frowned at that. There were tones to use to Princes, and this was not among them. His own voice turned hard.

"But I am not likely to lose my head over a wench," he said.

He stared at me, weak blue eyes narrowed in a spite that must always have lain hidden behind the flattery he showed me at my court.

"Nor burn harvest crops. Nor call a dwarf warrior, offending warriors of true human stock. Nor take another Prince's city as my own."

He watched me. Anger burned my mind, forging bitter words to answer him. But I held them back. I had offended him already. Offending him further might well be enough to earn me a place in his cells. And once in them, the Great alone knew when I would be freed.

So I said: "You are right, sire. I am punished for my faults."

His smile returned. He clapped his hands

and a polymuf brought another dish to the table.

"Try this meat, Perry. We have done well for boar this year."

I was shivering. "I am not hungry, sire."

Matthew leaned forward. "But I would have you eat."

There was no ally here, but a Prince I must obey. I took meat and forced myself to eat it.

Tired though I was I had little sleep that night. My thoughts were baying hounds that leaped round me, their stricken prey, savage and merciless. I tried to kill them, but from each blow they rose and gave louder tongue. And the hounds wore mocking faces: Harding, Blaine, Greene. Most of all, Edmund and Blodwen. They laughed at me and at each other; but the first was the laughter of scorn, the second of joy and desire.

And with this I sweated and shivered. In the morning my limbs were heavy and my head ached with a pain that throbbed behind my eyes. The shivering would not stop. Matthew noticed it when I went to pay my respects on departure. He asked:

"Are you well, Perry?"

"Well enough, sire."

"You do not look well. You are welcome to

stay longer, and I can have my surgeon sent to you. Or at least one of his assistants."

I gritted my teeth. My need to be clear of this man and his court put aside for a moment my other thoughts of hatred and revenge. I said:

"I am very well, sire. I will not trespass further on your kindness."

Hans when he saw me was alarmed. He too urged me to stay in Andover, at an inn if not at the palace. We had enough gold to pay for a lodging. But I would not listen to him; I had to be out in the open.

He said: "Do we make for Salisbury, sire?"

We had gone north, out of our direct way, to avoid Romsey land. I did not know what resentments lingered there and might be exercised against one who had conquered them as Prince but now was powerless.

"We ride that way," I said, "but we will not enter the city." He looked at me. "While I lack power I will stay away from cities."

"And in Sanctuary the Spirits will give you power?"

My head was light and heavy at the same time. I laughed.

"If they do not, I think no one else will!"

We were riding down the main street that led from the palace. Three black-robed figures walked the opposite way: the Seer of

Andover with two Acolytes. He saw me but affected not to know me, and I rode past with no salute. The Seers could do nothing for me at this point; and to have commerce with me would compromise them needlessly. Ezzard's fate was still remembered. It was because of this that I had left Winchester without seeing Grimm.

I rode on to the West Gate. My head throbbed with pain and anger. The Seers could do nothing for me. The High Seers in Sanctuary were a different matter.

The day was windless but the cold bit savagely and deep into the bone. The sky was dark gray with a shade of pink in it: full of snow. Some was shed during the morning. Small flakes, scarcely more than white dust, floated slow, slow, and specked the frozen ground. By midday the snow had stopped, but the sky above us looked ready to burst with it.

We stopped to eat at an inn high up in the hills. I had no hunger but forced myself to take something; not this time to suit another's whim but to keep up my strength. I knew now I had a fever. My forehead burned when I put up a hand to wipe it. I saw my Aunt Mary again, and heard her say: "Starve a fever, child . . ." All right for a child at home, I told her, tucked in a warm cot—a journey in this weather was a different matter. Hans said: "Sire?" and I realized I must have mumbled words aloud. "Nothing," I told him, and returned to my dish. It was a game pie, foul looking and foul tasting. I felt sick but chewed and swallowed as best I could.

We rode again, and the snow came down more thickly. The flakes were bigger and began to whirl in dance as the wind got up.

Hans pointed. "Is that not Amesbury, sire?" I nodded. "It might be best to take shelter there. It will be worse before long."

"No." I heard my voice buzz and echo. "We will pass to the south of it. We can reach Sanctuary by nightfall."

We came to the river and had to go south again, a long way south, to find a ford. The snow played a game with us, almost stopping and then blowing fierce in our faces. I felt giddy. My head at one moment was a bladder, which I feared might float off my shoulders and away among the snowflakes; the next a lump of aching lead.

I had been a fool not to do as Hans said. Snow covered the country all round us, obliterating landmarks. A fool in this, and in so many other things. Prince of Three Cities but two days since, and now . . . My teeth chattered in my burning head. Then the chattering and the burning and even the pain seemed to go far away, out into the flickering whiteness of the sky.

Hans cried: "Sire, are you all right?"

I could not answer him. I felt myself slipping from the saddle and tried to grip the rein, but my hand would not obey me. The whiteness all round turned to black.

The nightmare had many parts to it and many characters. Harding was there and I cursed him. I swore vengeance, and saw the vengeance taken. His head stared down from the palace gate and a crow plucked his eyes. Then that changed, and it was not the palace gate but the East Gate, and the head was my father's. I wept, and beside me Harding laughed. Then in fury I killed him again and butchered his body with my steel. And the bleeding corpse got up, and mocked me still.

Edmund was there, too. I rode with him by the Contest Field, and pleaded with him, for our friendship's sake, not to wrong me. He spoke me fair, but looked beyond me and smiled at someone else. I knew who it was that won a smile he had never given me.

Blodwen came to me alone. She stood on the stair above her father's throne room, and said: "I will be my own woman always. Remember that, Luke of Winchester. I will be my own woman." "Be what you will," I cried, "as long as you are mine!" "I will be my own woman, Luke of Winchester . . ." "Be that, but not his, not his . . ." She smiled, and I cried: "Swear you do not love him!" She shook her lovely head. "No. That I will not swear." "You are mine! Mine, and I shall have you." She shook her head again. "No. You never will. But it does not matter. It does not matter because you are dying, Luke, in the snow. Edmund has me, and you are dying, dying . . ."

Then it was over. My spirit floated in air, without substance, without organs, but I saw and heard. She and Edmund walked together in the palace garden, their fingers linked. They whispered and I heard their whispering. "Poor Luke, dead in the snow. Poor Luke." They laughed and, laughing, kissed.

My spirit winged like a bird, high over the city walls and across the blind white land. I hunted for my body, with one end in view. A body had an arm and an arm could hold a sword, and a sword would cut them down . . .

All this and more. Time had no meaning, any more than place or person. It went on endlessly, the taking and giving of pain. But at last there was quiet, and after the quiet, voices that neither jeered nor wept, but spoke evenly and with sense. I knew the voices, and knew this was no dream. I opened my eyes and there was whiteness here, too, but the whiteness of sheet and pillowslip. And I saw the broad wrinkled face of Murphy, the High Seer, clear in electric light.

He smiled. "How are you, Luke?"

"Well enough." I felt weak but the fever was gone. "How did I get here?"

"You have that dwarf of yours to thank."

"Hans? Is he well?"

"Yes. Since you were here last we have set up a television scanner on one of the standing stones. The barbarians press closer from the west all the time, and we cannot be sure they will recognize holy ground when they see it. We need to keep an eye open for visitors. But scarcely in a blizzard. Robb switched it on to make the routine test we carry out once a day. And to his astonishment he saw two horses coming up the hill through the snowstorm, with a dwarf mounted on one and a body strapped to the other. And as they neared the circle the snow cleared and he saw the body had a face he knew."

"Hans brought me here? That took courage."

"So I would think." Murphy chuckled. "You should have seen his face when the earth opened up in front of him!"

I thought of it. To have followed me to

Sanctuary would have been a great enough thing. I remembered my own fear when I first saw the Stones, enormous in the empty hillside, and that had been on a fair day, with Ezzard the Seer guiding me. To have ridden up into the dread circle through a snowstorm, leading my horse with me unconscious or even dead on its back . . . I had been right to make him warrior. I did not think there was another in my army who could have done it.

My army . . . I said:

"He has told you what happened—or what he knows of it?"

"We knew already," Murphy said. "From Grimm."

Of course. Pigeons might not fly in a blizzard, but nothing stopped the invisible radio waves which bound the Seers in the cities to the High Seers in Sanctuary.

"I have served you and your cause," I said. "Now I come to you for help."

"You were right to do so."

"I want . . ."

I started to rise from the bed but weakness made me fall back. Murphy said:

"There will be plenty of time to talk of what you want. Get your strength back first."

"Is Hans . . . ?"

"We had difficulty in getting him from

your bedside but in the end tiredness over-
came him. He is sleeping. You need to do the
same."

It was two days later, days marked by electric clocks, not by the rising and setting of the
sun—that I spoke to the High Seers together.
We sat in the big room whose walls were
painted with landscapes, a trick to deceive the
mind into thinking we were not underground
but looking out through windows at the living earth. I do not know about the High Seers
but my mind was not deceived. It made me
miss the reality all the more.

But the High Seers, perhaps, having lived
in this way so long, had grown used to it. And
they had their mission, compared with which
nothing else mattered. I looked at them:
Lanark, Murphy, Robb, Gunter and the rest.
They wore no formal robes but ordinary sim-
ple clothes, and their heads were not cropped.
There was nothing to remark on in them.
Nothing except the knowledge they held and
hoped to restore; and the power that knowledge gave.

They put questions to me and I answered
them as patiently as I could. Murphy said:

"It is a setback. There is no denying it. But
there are favorable possibilities. This Eric of

Oxford, who looks for change. He is only Prince in Waiting, but we may be able to do something about that. Lukis is Seer in Oxford . . ."

I interrupted him. "'I am sure there are intrigues that can be woven. But I did not come for this."

Murphy started to speak again but old Lanark put a hand up to stop him. He said:

"Let Luke speak."

I tapped the sword in my belt. There was no need for it here but I wore it. Perhaps it did for me what the painted walls did for the High Seers. What tricks the mind is what the mind is glad to be tricked by.

"You gave me this," I said, "the Sword of the Spirits. I killed my brother with it and took the city which you had planned I should have. But the city is lost to us now, and no sword will win it back. I need another weapon."

They were silent, watching me.

"Our ancestors had weapons which killed at a distance. They called them firearms. You know of them and can make them for me."

Robb said: "You would still need an army. One man cannot conquer a city even with firearms."

"I will get an army."

"From Oxford?" Murphy said. He shook his head. "Even if Eric were Prince he could not put guns in the hands of his army. There more than in most places their minds are closed against such things, but there is not a city throughout the civilized lands where men would accept them."

"Not in the civilized lands," I said. "but there is a city. The Prince at night watches a cinematograph film. They cut grass with machines and have crossbows to drive arrows. His Chancellor is polymuf."

"Klan Gothlen? It lies very far away. And what makes you think that Prince would help you? His daughter is in Winchester, and your enemy."

"He owes me a debt."

"Debts are not always paid."

"One can seek payment."

Murphy shrugged, in doubt. But Lanark said:

"This may offer something. There is no harm in trying in that quarter as well as at Oxford. We could send someone north in the spring, and see how the land lies."

"The weapon," I said. "You could give me such a thing?"

Lanark said to Robb: "Do you have a film to show us?"

"I think I can find what you want."

While he was getting the film and others set up screen and projector, I said to Lanark:

"I thought I might find Martin here. He arrived safely?"

Lanark nodded. "And went on."

"Went on? Where?"

"To the other Sanctuary. In the ruins of London."

"You sent him there?"

"No. It was his choice."

"What is it he is seeking?"

"I do not know," Lanark said, "but he did not find it here."

Robb ran the film. It was not like that scratched and jerky picture of comic animals which I had seen at Cymru's court. What one saw, unlike the paintings on the wall, looked almost real enough to touch. Men walked across a field, a line of fifty or more of them. They walked easily, talking and laughing. Then one saw other men, a few only, waiting in a thicket at the field's end. They carried long tubes of metal, with a triangle at the end and something sticking down underneath. They raised the triangles to their shoulders and put their hands round the part beneath. Harsh and savage sound, the stammering of tongueless giants, broke out. And the line of men fell, sinking like wheat to the sickle's sweep.

Robb switched off the projector and put up the room lights. He said:

"Is that the sort of thing you want?"

I was amazed and shocked, but I said: "Yes. And they can be made? Not just one, but many?"

Robb was a short thin man, with a skin even more pallid than the other High Seers. He wore spectacles with lenses of thick glass. He said:

"Many of our ancestors' weapons were complex things, but this is not. They called it the Sten gun. It can be made fairly easily."

"Can it be used on horseback?"

"Probably. But a man on foot would control it better."

Lanark said: "You say the sword we gave you is no longer enough, Luke, that you need a far more powerful weapon. You may be right. But you must understand that other changes follow the changes of weapons. Horses are bigger targets against guns than men on foot. When the Sten gun returns there will be no more riding into battle."

I nodded, scarcely listening, seeing my enemies—Harding, Blaine, Edmund and the rest—struck down in their triumph and laughter.

"There is another thing," Lanark said. "You are a man of Winchester. You found it hard to believe that Blaine could put swords into the hands of the Wilsh to fight his own people. Will you take a whole army of Wilsh against your city, and with weapons such as these? Do you think you can?"

I saw the council of Captains with their hands raised against me. And I remembered Edmund and Blodwen in the dream, whispering, laughing, kissing.

I said: "Have no fear, Lanark. I will do it."

7

The People of the Bells

Hans, after the first shock, accustomed himself well to life in Sanctuary and to the wonders the High Seers showed him. He watched them at work in the laboratories, and put questions which they answered. Apart from the power it might give, this science of theirs had small interest to me. It was not so with Hans. Although his chief passion had been to serve as a warrior, rather than be an armorer like his father, he came of a long line of metal-working craftsmen. Once he had accepted the idea of machines he saw easily enough how they worked. The High Seers were ready to instruct him, and he was quick to learn.

Robb and a man called Kinnell were the ones principally concerned with the Sten gun.

I listened when Hans spoke to them but made little sense of it. There was talk of cordite, of percussion caps, of blow-back open-bolt action —and a dozen other things which to me meant nothing. All I was aware of was the gun itself taking shape. I gazed at it as a hungry man might watch a rabbit roasting, tantalized and impatient.

At last it was finished and we gathered in one of the storerooms to see it work. A target was set up at the far end. Robb showed me how to hold the gun and press the trigger. I lifted it and fired. I felt it jerk, almost like a living thing, and the noise of the tongueless stammering giant echoed in the room. And the target showed a ragged line of holes.

Until now, despite the ancient film they had shown me, I had not really believed in the power of this weapon. But it was no longer possible to doubt. I lowered the gun and said:

"You have done well, Robb."

"It is not so accurate as other weapons of the past," he said. "And the range is no more than about two hundred yards."

"Two hundred yards is enough. Give me a hundred of them, fifty even, and no army will stand against me."

Robb laughed. "We chose this gun because it was the simplest to make, but it still needs making! And we have no more than two hands apiece. Fifty, you say? By next autumn, perhaps, but I would not guarantee it."

"Autumn! I need them long before that."

"You are impatient, Luke," Lanark said, "and we understand why. But things must take their time. It is not only a question of guns. You have an army to find as well. We must wait till winter ends before we can sound out the Wilsh King. And then our messenger will need to go about it warily."

"It is I who must ask it of Cymru."

"And chance being sent back to Winchester with your hands roped behind you? Or maybe executed on the spot for the insult to his daughter? It would be an absurd risk to take. No, Luke, this is something you must leave to us."

I spoke to Hans next morning when he came to clean my room.

The High Seers had no servants, except for the machines invented by our ancestors to ease house labor. Each looked after himself, even old Lanark. But Hans would have none of this. It was not proper, he said, for a Prince to do such things. The High Seers laughed, but Hans paid no heed and continued to serve me. And I accepted the service, knowing that to reject it would be an insult.

So I watched while he used the machine that cleaned the floor, sucking up dirt and dust. It made a whining noise as it moved, a scream of protest such as one would never have heard from a polymuf. At last he switched it off and it was possible to speak. And for once we were alone with none to hear what passed between us.

I said: "This Sten gun, Hans—you have watched the making and listened to what Robb and Kinnell said of it?"

"Yes, sire."

"And understood?" He nodded. "You could make such a thing yourself? The bullets also? And teach others to do the same?"

"Yes. It would not be difficult, as long as one could get the materials. For cordite one needs gun cotton and nitroglycerine. Gun cotton itself requires sulphuric and nitric acids . . ."

I cut him short. "It means nothing to me. What matters is that it does to you. The Wilsh would have these things? Or could get them?"

"Yes. It would be no more difficult than making the asbestos cloth, out of chrysotile, which the peddler used to cross the Burning Lands."

"And therefore their craftsmen could make these Sten guns?"

"Yes." He nodded. "Even though most of them are not dwarfs, they do not lack skill."

"Good! That is what I hoped to hear. Hans, I think it is time we went on another journey."

"To Klan Gothlen? But the High Seers forbid it."

"They had me penned in once before," I said, "for the greater part of a winter. But I was a boy then. I did not come here to be treated like a boy again."

"Sire," he said earnestly, "hear me. There is wisdom in what they say. If you go to Cymru, he may imprison or even kill you. They are a strange people, the Wilsh. They smile easily, but they are good haters too. And the lady Blodwen meant much to them."

"I will take that chance."

"And it is high winter. And we have no horses. Those on which we came were sent to the Seer's stable at Amesbury."

All this was true and made sense. Few traveled in the winter, and then no farther than to the next city. Earlier that morning I had looked through the television scanner and seen nothing but a white whirling wilderness. It made no difference. I said:

"Will you come with me, Hans, if I ask you?"

He looked at me. "You know it, sire."

The blizzard raged two days more. The morning after the snow stopped we left Sanctuary before anyone else was stirring. I pressed the button on the top landing of the staircase and the trap door opened over our heads, creaking more than usual under its weight of snow. Some of the snow scattered down on us. It brought with it the cold sting of fresh air and I drew deep breath to fill my lungs.

During those two days, taking care not to be observed, Hans had packed rucksacks for us, with food and other things we would need on the journey. He had also made us snowshoes, such as peasants wear to cross their fields in winter, using plastic instead of the usual strips of hide in a wooden frame. They were oval in shape, about a foot long, and had straps that buckled over our boots.

Even so the going was hard. I was not used to walking; even to go from the palace to the River Road I would have taken horse. And although the shoes prevented one's feet from sinking below the surface, the snow dragged at them. It was not long before the muscles at the backs of my legs were aching from the strain, and within an hour I had to call a halt to rest. Hans fared better: a dwarf is more strongly muscled in the leg and he had used his more.

I had forgotten also how much wider the world is to a man on foot than it is to a horseman. One would see a mark in the distance and reckon ten minutes as the time needed to reach it. Half an hour later it would seem scarcely nearer. The monotony of the trudging was worse than the fatigue; my muscles accustomed themselves to the strain sooner than my mind did.

We were nearly three days getting to the pass that crossed the Burning Lands. We avoided towns and villages, where travelers at this season would excite interest, but did stay one night at an isolated farm. I told a story of a pilgrimage imposed by the Seer on account of an unwitting act of impiety toward the Spirits. They accepted this but expressed surprise that a dwarf should be my servant. Hans accounted for it by telling them he was not a dwarf but polymuf, with marks on his body beneath his clothes. It must have cost him dearly in pride to do so.

The second night we found a deserted hut and slept there. And in the afternoon of the third day we came to the dead landscape lying under the hills of the Burning Lands, where snow gave way to black rock and steaming pools. We took off our snowshoes and started on the last mile or two leading to the pass.

I had thought winter might have chilled

the black sand underfoot and made our crossing easier, but it seemed to have had no effect on it. We had each brought three extra pairs of boots, changing them as they got too hot, but we scorched our feet all the same. We crossed, however, and soaked our legs in a tepid pool while our last pairs of boots cooled off. They had suffered badly; and we still had something like two hundred miles of rough and wintry country to travel.

At least it no longer mattered who saw us. We found a village before nightfall, a primitive place but with a cobbler who, for gold, sat up all night and had new boots ready for us in the morning. Hans shook his head over the workmanship—they were poor objects by our Winchester standards—but they would serve.

So we went north, taking much the same route as we had taken under Greene's command when the peddler guided us. But that had been in spring and on horseback. Now we plodded over fields of snow, wearily through a barren world. We saw few animals, rabbits or an occasional hare, its ears pricked in silhouette against the white skyline, slinking foxes, ermine, once a wild boar. I would have welcomed a change from the dried meat we had brought with us. Given a horse and spear I could have run it down easily. I thought of the Sten gun, which would have killed it more easily still, and put my hand to where it hung at my belt. But though we had brought several magazines of bullets, I would not use it. We must make do with the rations we had.

At last we reached the river whose valley we had followed before. Fresh blizzards sprang up soon after, but we found shelter in a village. We stayed two days, in a stinking hut with stinking savages, taking turns to sleep at night in case one of them seized an opportunity to cut our throats. Though I doubt if there was any real danger of it. They were a cowed lot, undernourished and of poor physique, and they seemed to regard us with fear. All the same I was glad when we could go on.

The river was frozen and there were marks on the fresh snow that covered it, showing where animals had crossed. Some of the prints were very large, much bigger than those of a man, and made, I realized when I studied them, by some creature that walked upright as a man does. Whatever it may have been, we did not see it.

Although the snow had stopped, the wind remained strong and a little west of north. It blew in our faces on the valley floor and we went up onto higher ground where pine trees covering the ridge offered some protection. It was from these trees, in mid-afternoon, that the attack came.

I was not looking that way and my first awareness arose from Hans' cry of alarm. We were some ten yards apart—he had stopped to tighten a strap on his snowshoes while I plodded on—and I looked back to see long dark shapes racing down the slope toward him. I barely had time to recognize them as huge dogs, a dozen or more, before they reached him. The leader leaped in a great arc, covering many feet of intervening space. Hans put up his arms in defense, but the beast's weight smashed him to the ground.

Others were on him as he fell. They had swept down from the trees in silence but now they gave savage tongue. Half of them were mauling Hans and the rest ran on toward me. I lifted the Sten gun, not bothering to aim, and fired at them. One fell; at once the others turned tail.

Those attacking Hans retreated also. I went to him and helped him to rise. He was bleeding heavily from bites on the arms, whch he had used to protect his face and throat from their teeth. I let go my support of him and he moaned and fell. I saw then that the blood was also gushing from his right leg.

I tore up a linen shirt from my pack and set to work to bind up the wounds. That in the leg was the ugliest, a long tear exposing bloody muscle and sinew. It was plain that, tough as he was, he would not be able to stand, let alone walk.

I looked up the snow slope to the line of trees. Shapes skulked there, watchful. One howled, and others followed suit. Their presence being known, there was no need for silence.

We had been told of these creatures by the peddler. They were polyhounds who hunted in packs and, like the building rats, showed signs of more intelligence than a beast should have. A troop of horse such as we then were would be unlikely to encounter them, the peddler said. They watched for people traveling alone or in small groups.

Probably they had been silently tracking us for some time, and had attacked when they could surprise us separated from one another. It was a further indication, both of their cunning and their ferocity, that although the Sten gun had caused an immediate retreat they had not gone far.

They were still much too near for comfort. I got Hans to take a hold round my neck and staggered, carrying him on my back, down toward the valley floor. When we had covered twenty or thirty yards, he said:

"They are coming after us."

I set him down and fired at them again, and again they retreated into the line of trees. This happened several times, and I scored a hit on one of them at least; it limped away howling and dripping blood on the snow. But the time came when they did not go back as far as the trees. Instead they moved out and round, making a great circle which had us as its center. I tasted fear in my throat, understanding what had happened: by trial and error they had estimated the Sten gun's range and taken up positions outside it.

The valley was white and empty, apart from us and the surrounding polyhounds. From time to time there were bursts of howling; but their silences were more chilling still. I remembered something else the peddler had said: although hunger might sometimes drive them to attack by day, they were reckoned far more dangerous by night. Already the afternoon was fading into dusk.

I carried Hans, and rested, and carried him again. The polyhounds kept pace and distance, moving when we moved and stopping when we stopped. Progress was arduous, and painfully slow. Hans said at last:

"Sire, you must leave me and go on."

We had covered scarcely a quarter of a mile. I said, panting:

"It is true, I might find help. There was a

village where the river forked—do you remember? It cannot be more than a few miles
north. I could bring men back with me."

Hans looked up from where he crouched in
the snow.

"Yes. I will be all right till then."

I handed him the gun. He tried to refuse it,
but I said:

"They know we can wound or kill them
from a distance. Therefore they will keep
clear of both of us while it is light. But after
that you may need to hold them off for a time.
I will return as quickly as I can."

I set off before he could make further protest. The polyhounds also moved. Half followed me while the rest kept their places
around Hans. I went a hundred yards, a hundred and fifty. Then Hans' voice came to me,
urgently shouting:

"Back, sire! Come back!"

I had already seen it: the ones that had followed me were closing in. They moved to
head me off as I doubled back. I saw one
brute loping in toward me and cursed the
hampering snowshoes I wore, though I would
have been little better off without them. He
must intercept me. But the Sten gun chattered and he dropped with a scream of pain.
The others fell away and I reached Hans.

It took me some moments to gather breath to speak.

"Cunning indeed," I said. "They know there is only one gun, and saw me give it to you."

"You must take it," Hans said. "And you must go on. The gun is only to use while there is light. After that, nothing will stop them."

The polyhounds had taken up the same circle as before, just out of range. I said:

"I will get some of them, even in the dark."

"But it serves no purpose, sire. Remember, you have a mission."

A mission? He meant, of course, the task laid on me by the High Seers. As if that mattered compared with the life of someone who had twice saved mine. But there was something else, deep in the darkness of my mind. Hans was right in saying that I could not save him by staying: I would only lose my own life along with his. Yet it was not that which filled me with despair and bitterness. It was the thought of dying with my revenge unaccomplished.

I think he read uncertainty in my face. He said:

"Go, sire. You must do your duty as a Prince. Nothing else matters."

I had left him before in the hope of bringing back help. There was nothing like this now; they would be on him, tearing him to pieces, as soon as I was gone. I shook my head, to clear the black madness from it. I said harshly:

"I am staying, Hans. That is a Prince's duty; and a friend's."

I looked past him to the polyhounds. They had ceased their howling and were silent. They seemed to be listening to something. There was no sound but that of our breathing and the wind's distant sighing in the pines. Or was there a noise, faint and far off? I strained my ears and heard it. Scarcely audible, it rose and fell with the gusting wind: a tiny jangling tinkle of bells.

The polyhounds had heard it, too. They barked, one to another like men in council. Then the circle was broken as they ran round us to re-form their pack on the slope above. They ran, silent again, into the cover of trees and disappeared.

I saw figures come into view, bearing down the slope from the north, below the tree line. They were men, but traveling so fast over the snow that I wondered if some sort of machine carried them. But as they came nearer I saw that they were sliding on long thin planks. I waved and shouted and they changed course, dipping down the valley's side toward us.

They were more than a score in number. They were dressed in furs and looked strong and healthy, well nourished. They greeted us amiably and asked what help we needed.

I told them of the polyhounds and they nodded. They often warred with these beasts and had their measure. One of them, smiling, tapped a wicked-looking knife in his belt and showed a fur cap with half a dozen polyhound tails dangling from it.

They had ropes, and made a litter to carry Hans. Some went on down the valley, moving fast on the thin planks which they called skis, but the rest accompanied us at our slower pace. We traveled south a couple of miles; then west up a side valley. Their village was there. The huts were stoutly built of wood. Blue smoke rose from chimneys and there was an appetizing smell of food cooking.

People came out to greet us. These too were healthy and had smiling faces. The women took Hans and saw to his wounds, replacing my rough bandages with others of clean linen, smeared with a healing ointment. Others poured hot spiced ale into pots for the returning hunters, and for me also.

Unlike that other village in which we had

stayed, this one was pleasant, and so were its inhabitants. There were many items one could note: the stoutness and cleanliness of the huts, the signs of good husbandry and prosperity—bins brimming with fat corn, smoked hams and sides of salmon hanging from the roof beams—the comeliness of both men and women, the vigor and merriness of the children. But I felt there was more to it than the sum of these parts. There was a sense of warmth and ease which went deep. It was not quite like anything I had known.

I was concerned at first about their reaction to the Sten gun. Either they might, as would have been the case in the lands of the south, regard it as an evil thing and Hans and me as deserving of death for possessing it; or they might covet it for its power. But neither was the case. They looked at it with scarcely even curiosity, and no desire for possession.

They were altogether strangely incurious. I told them, in explanation of how we got there, that we came from the south and were traveling to Klan Gothlen and the court of King Cymru. They nodded, indicating that they had heard of the city and the king, but asked no other questions.

It was plain that we must stay with them for some days, while Hans' wounds healed. I offered gold for our lodging. They glanced at the coins with as little interest as they had shown in the Sten gun, and handed them back. Hospitality needed no payment. They might have added, but did not, that in any case they had no use for gold.

During the days that followed I came to know them, and their way of life, better. There was one man, older and bigger than the rest, to whom—it seemed to me—some deference was paid. I guessed he was their chief, and addressed him as such. He denied it, smiling. His name was Jok, and he had no title. None of them did. They had heard of kings and chiefs and such, but there was none here.

I did not believe him at first, thinking it some pretense of modesty or custom. I asked who made decisions among them. He said the Tribe did. But what, I asked, if the Tribe were divided among itself? Jok laughed. That could not be! One might as well speak of a man's left arm being divided from his right.

This did not convince me. I did not see how any group of people could live together without dissension, always in agreement. It made no sense. But as time passed, though I looked for discord among them, I found none.

They had no marriage as such, and no paternity. The children were children of the Tribe, not of a particular couple. They called all women Mother, all men Father. In a similar fashion those of adult years, when they did not use given names, called each other Brother and Sister.

Most of the things they did seemed to follow one person's prompting, the rest falling in with whatever notion was put forward. Nor was it always the same person, or group of people, who suggested things. It was almost as though they thought with a single mind, so that it did not matter whose voice it was first uttered any project.

The men were hunters; the women cooked and cleaned for them and cared for the sick and old and, of course, the children. In summer, men and women worked together in the fields, sharing the labor of sowing and planting and harvesting. I saw there were no polymufs or dwarfs among them, and asked about that. I was told they were smothered at birth. This was not out of revulsion or in obedience to the behest of Spirits, but from kindness. It would be cruel, they felt, to let a crippled child live, different from his brothers and sisters and deprived of the fullness of activity which they enjoyed.

And what, I asked, if a man or woman were crippled later in life: in the hunt, perhaps? Again it was Jok I was talking to, and he shook his head. Such a person would be well cared for, in hope of recovery. Should the time come when he knew he would not regain his true strength, he would bid farewell to the Tribe and leave the village. There was an herb growing in the woods which brought a quiet death.

The whole village was a place of cheerful noise. They talked and laughed much, and apart from that there were the bells. They had a passion for them. They wore small bells on their clothes, and larger ones hung outside the huts, to jangle with each puff of wind, and inside on intricate arrangements of cords which could be agitated by the touch of a hand or even by the chance pressure of a footstep. They were so delicately balanced that they would go on sounding long afterward.

Hans' wounds healed fast: perhaps because of the ointment the women put on them and perhaps to some extent through the happiness and contentment we found here. I had often heard it said that a wound stays angry when a warrior has an angry wife. It may be the opposite is true also.

The days passed easily. I practiced wearing these skis of theirs and in due course went out with the men to hunt, following clumsily and falling a lot in the snow but managing on the whole to keep up with them. We killed deer and boar, stabbing them with long sharp knives—even in deep winter this was good country for game. (While hunting they silenced the bells they wore with strips of cloth.) We saw the tracks and spoor of polyhounds, too, but the trails were old ones.

One night, having watched the women see to Hans' leg, I said to Jok:

"He is well enough to travel. It is time we bade you farewell."

He was silent and I did not think he had heard me: the tintinnabulation of the bells was very noisy. I started to repeat myself but he said:

"I was not born of the Tribe."

It did not seem to have anything to do with my own remark but I listened politely. He went on:

"Sometimes strangers are accepted among us. I was such a stranger once."

I still did not take his drift and remained silent. He looked at me, smiling:

"Stay with us, Luke."

I was astonished. I said: "It is a kindness and an honor. But should not the rest of your people be consulted?"

He laughed. "Do you know us so little yet? Each speaks for all."

I said awkwardly: "Then I am grateful for the offer. But I cannot stay."

"Why not? You are happy here."

He spoke with calmness and certainty. And

there was more to it than the words by themselves might convey. He meant also that among his people a man would know happiness of a kind that he would find in no other place; and wild though the boast might seem I could not disbelieve it.

I said: "And Hans?"

"He, as well."

"A dwarf?"

"We would not keep a babe so stunted, but he has grown to manhood. His legs are short but his body is strong. We welcome Hans also."

I shook my head. "It is no good. I must go on."

"For what reason?"

At last he was curious—curious that any should refuse the gift of their comradeship. I hesitated. The hopes and plans of the High Seers would make no sense to him—they meant little enough to me at this moment. So I said nothing of that, but spoke of the wrongs I had suffered: of friendship and trust betrayed, that city lost which was mine by right. Jok listened. At last he said:

"We can heal you of this sickness, Luke."

"Sickness? I am not sick."

"Very sick. Those who have been born in the Tribe would not understand you, but I do. I remember things like jealousy and pride and hatred of one's fellow man. Or woman. They are distant memories, almost forgotten but not quite. The Tribe healed me, and can heal you. Already these wrongs you fancy were done you are less important: is that not true?"

I could not deny it. During recent days I had scarcely thought of Edmund and Blodwen and Harding. My nights had been unbroken, my dreams happy.

"Stay with us," Jok said. "Forget your ambitions and angers. We have much to give you: an end to loneliness and misery, a peace of heart such as you can only guess at now."

That too was true. Even after this short time of living with them I knew it to be so. It was absurd on the face of it that I, who had been Prince of three cities, should be tempted by the thought of living, with neither rank nor glory, among a primitive tribe of hutdwellers; but I was tempted. To forget all wretchedness of the past, for the first time in my life to be at peace . . .

But I summoned up two faces, hers and his, and summoned my resolution with it. I said harshly:

"You mean well, and I thank you for it. But it does not serve my purpose."

"No?" He put his hand on mine, the touch in itself a token of all he had promised.

"Then stay only for a few days longer. Your revenge will wait."

It would wait, but waiting it might die, withered by this warmth of giving and sharing. And I knew that in my deepest heart nothing—no peace or happiness or goodness—counted with me as this did.

I said: "We leave tomorrow."

"So be it." He shook his head slightly. "We could have healed you. Go in what peace you can know. Maybe in the end you will heal yourself; but you will suffer for it."

Since Klan Gothlen was a city without walls, there was no guard to challenge us as we entered it. We walked through the streets, with the domed and spired and turreted buildings rising on either side, their colors looking more gaudy still against the snowy hills beyond. People looked at us with interest as we passed, but that meant nothing. The Wilsh were always inquisitive about new things, new faces. Dirty and travel-worn as we were, it was scarcely likely that we would be recognized as Luke, the slayer of the Bayemot, and his servant Hans.

The guard on the palace did not know me either until I spoke. Then he dropped his spear and let me through. I asked a footman

where I would find the King, and he told me
in the red chamber. He would have an-
nounced me but I told him I would find my
own way there. He bowed and stood aside: my
reputation was still a passport in this place. I
wondered how much longer that would be
true.

It was warm after the cold outside: too
warm. I remembered Cymru telling me that
in winter they heated the floors with fires that
warmed air beneath them. Within moments I
was sweating. At the door of the red chamber
I was challenged again, and passed again. I
went through into a hum of talk, which
stopped on my appearance.

Cymru was there, lying among cushions on
a couch of crimson velvet matching the crimson of the wall hangings. I saw many others I
knew: Kluellan, the Colonel of the Guard,
Snake, Cymru's polymuf Chancellor with ten-
tacles for fingers and strangely jointed limbs,
Bevili, the Perfumer Royal with his scarlet
lips . . . a dozen or more nobles of the city.
Snake was the first to address me. He said:

"Luke of Winchester! So our hero returns.
But you look as though you have had a hard
journey here."

I had, I knew, offended against Wilsh etiquette by coming into the King's presence

dirty and disheveled. But it seemed to me this was no occasion for etiquette. I eased the pack from my shoulders and let it drop.

Cymru said: "What brings you to us in the full of winter? And in such a state?" He raised himself from his cushions and stared at me. His dark face had no smile of welcome. "Where is Blodwen?"

"In Winchester, sire."

He frowned. "You have left her there, unguarded?"

"I had no choice."

His eyes went small. "Do you say so? We put her into your protection."

"Will you hear me, sire?"

Cymru said grimly: "We will hear you."

I told my story, sparing nothing. Cymru and the Wilsh nobles watched me as I spoke. There was shock and amazement in their faces but I could not read what else. When I finished there was a pause before Cymru spoke.

"You have lost your city," he said, "and you have lost Blodwen to one of those Captains who deposed you. What brings you here? Do you seek an audience for your tears? Or perhaps a pension?"

"Neither, sire. I seek an army."

His cold eyes studied me and he pulled his grizzled beard.

"You beg our aid?"

I shook my head. "I beg nothing, sire. I demand it."

"Demand?" He was incredulous. "Of me?"

"She was your gift," I said, "in return for slaying the Bayemot. I gave you thanks. I took her in good faith. She played me false and, through her, enemies have stolen my city from me. In breaking faith with me she dishonors you, and all your people. She is your daughter, Cymru. I demand your aid so that I may kill her and her lover."

His face had changed while I was saying this. Coldness and surprise gave way to heat and anger. By the time I finished it was full of rage. He would have me killed, I thought, and vowed I would not die quietly. I would take some of them with me, perhaps Cymru himself, before they cut me down.

But the rage and anger were not for me. He said:

"All you say is truth. You will have your army. And I will ride with you when you go to take your revenge."

8

The Battle of Amesbury

From that moment Blodwen's name was never mentioned in Cymru's court. They were good haters, the Wilsh. I remember what Blodwen herself had said, as she rode between Edmund and me on the day of the hunt, the day of the killing of the Baye-mot. "In our country when a man makes an enemy it is forever." She was Cymru's only child. He had loved her and indulged her greatly. But she had dishonored him, and that was enough. I think he would have watched her die with a smile on his lips.

Snake told me, and I believed him, that my own life had hung by a thread in the red room that afternoon. Had I shown weakness, he said, Cymru would have ordered my death because of the news I brought. I would have been a reminder of his disgrace, to be removed without pity.

But his acceptance of my vow to take revenge, and his joining with me in it, set me even higher in his regard than during my first visit to Klan Gothlen. Snake told me this also, before I had truly realized it.

"She was his daughter," he said, "but he would wash his hands in her blood. He would have killed you had you begged or flinched; and now you are his son. I do not say it lightly. Fond as he was of her, that is a lack he has always felt, and you fill it. No man who is wise will cross Luke of Winchester in this city from now on." He smiled. "It would be almost as bad as defying the King himself."

He spoke without rancor. He was a devious man, as I suppose a Chancellor should be, but I had come to respect him. His manner showed no resentment but no false flattery either. Behind the slyness of the surface he showed the world, there was some honesty.

And the truth of his forecast of my preeminence in the King's favor was borne out the next day. I was talking of the new tactics that would be required with the use of Sten guns, and Kluellan interrupted. He took something I said as showing ignorance of the qualities of Wilsh troops, and indignantly challenged what he thought was a slur. As

Colonel of the Guard he commanded the army in the field, directly under the King, and thought himself its spokesman. I held my peace, but Cymru said:

"Enough, Kluellan! You are older than Luke, but can learn from him." Others were present: Captains and civilian nobles. He raised his voice. "Luke is my lieutenant in this enterprise. I would have that kept in mind by all of you."

As I had guessed would be the case, the Wilsh were not shocked by the weapon I had brought them, but fascinated. At the demonstration I gave they clapped and shouted with delight. I had had a wooden target set up, but this did not satisfy Cymru. Snake, with his usual care for his monarch's future pleasures, had arranged for wild boar to be caught and kept in pens within the city; so that whenever the weather should prove fair enough to tempt Cymru to a hunt there would be quarry to be released. Cymru called for one of these to be loosed now, at the end of the narrow yard in which we stood.

It was a half-grown boar, not polybeast as far as I could see. It stood in front of the trap from which it had been set free, undecided what to do, alarmed probably by the noisy chatter of the Wilsh nobles.

"Now, Luke," Cymru cried, "show us what this gun of your does to that young tusker."

Except for food, one killed beasts only in sport; and there was no sport in firing bullets into a defenseless and most likely frightened animal. It was not even moving. But I remembered that Cymru's idea of a hunt was firing crossbow bolts from behind wooden covers. And it was Cymru I relied on to help get me back my city and my pride. I wasted no time in hesitation but raised the Sten gun to my waist and fired a burst. The boar gave one sharp squeal as the bullets smashed it to the ground, then lay there silent in its gore.

The Wilsh nobles broke into loud applause. Many, even ladies, rushed forward to examine the dead animal, and I saw one lady dabble her delicate fingers in its blood. I hid my disgust. These were my people until I won my own city back.

Cymru said: "Have it taken to Lewin." That was the Master Cook. "We will dine on roast boar tonight. Tell him I shall require one of his best sauces to go with it."

Hans turned armorer; and I wondered what old Rudi would have thought of it, recalling his regret when Hans, his last son, chose not to follow him to the forge. It was, of course, a very different kind of armory. In the King's name I had put Hans in complete charge of the making of the Sten guns. He was in any case the only man who had the knowledge for it. I could use the weapon, but I could as easily have flown up to the top of one of the Wilsh mountains as make it.

He found good and willing craftsmen here: not only dwarfs but polymufs and true men also. When I visited them in the forge-house I found a great bustle of activity, with the roar of flame and the clang and hammer of steel added to by a clamor of voices. Unlike our Winchester dwarfs, who were silent workers for the most part, the Wilsh could not even shape steel without chattering; and there were times when, one of them first taking up a tune, they would all burst out into singing.

I asked him one day how matters were progressing. He said:

"Very well, sire. They are quick to learn."

"By spring . . ."

"We shall have two hundred and fifty guns for you. More maybe. And ammunition enough and to spare. Will that do?"

"It will do. Hans, without you I could do nothing. These Wilsh soldiers are better than I once thought, but with equal weapons they would have small chance against our warriors of Winchester, and there are other territories to get through first. I think all the cities will fight against an army that comes from beyond the Burning Lands, whether it offers defiance or no."

Hans looked at me. "I think so, too, sire."

"I made you a warrior," I said, "and now you have become my armorer to help me. It will not be for long. When spring comes and the guns are ready you can be a warrior again. And this time one of my Captains."

I had thought he would be overjoyed. For a dwarf to be a warrior was a marvelous thing; but this would make him noble.

He said slowly: "It is a great honor, sire. But . . ."

I was amazed. "But what?"

"I am not sure I desire it."

His doubts did not stem from lack of courage, as I well knew. He had as brave a heart as any man I had met.

I said: "Why, Hans? Because you would be commanding Wilsh, against our own people?"

"No. I serve you against anyone. And I am making guns to kill them."

"Then why?"

He picked a Sten gun up and gazed at it. "I cannot remember a time when I did not want to be a warrior. There was a place where I could climb the citadel wall and stay there hidden, watching the drilling and jousting

and sword play. The longing was greater because it was an impossible thing."

He put the gun down and looked at me.

"By your hand, sire, the impossible became
a reality. I fought with you at Petersfield and
Romsey. But that was in the old way, on
horseback, with sword and shield. It will not
be the same to carry a gun at one's hip and
kill a man a hundred yards away—a man
maybe who has not even seen you. I will make
the guns but I do not think I want to use
them."

"You will not refuse to go with me when
we ride south, Hans?"

"No, sire." He smiled. "I will not do that.
Not then or ever. I go wherever you go."

I worked hard that winter, drilling and
organizing the army, making plans and prepa-
rations for the campaign to come. I rose early
and rested little through a long day. This was
no hardship. In work I could forget my
shames, and keep at bay those specters that
otherwise filled vacancy to mock and jeer at
me. There were hours on end when I did not
think of Blodwen, nights when I went to bed
so tired that I did not dream.

Cymru remonstrated with me for this un-
ceasing labor, though I think he was im-

pressed by it. He asked me to take things more easily, then begged, at last commanded. This was at the Christmas Feast, which the Wilsh kept far more lavishly even than we had done in Winchester. For twelve days there was a round of feasts and balls, masques and concerts and visitings, a vast gluttony of eating and drinking. Lewin and his minions produced mountains of food, most elaborately prepared, glazed and sauced. On one great table he set up a pyramid, ten feet high, of meats cooked and carved in strange patterns of shape and hue, the whole thing topped by the head of the biggest boar I had ever seen. A polybeast, of course, but that counted for nothing in this land.

On the chief day of the Feast there was a procession of Christians through the streets of the city, ending up at their church, a huge building bearing no fewer than seven large onion domes, which they called the Cathedral. Cymru and his court joined in the procession as it passed the palace and walked the last hundred yards with it, before actually going into the church immediately behind the Bishop.

When Cymru told me of this, taking it for granted that I would go with them, I said in surprise:

"But you are not a Christian."

"I am not one of the White Witches, either, but I attend their grand coven at midsummer. And preside at the feast the farmers give at harvest, though I am not a farmer. Amongst us the King is father to his people as long as they obey the law. And the Christians do that as well as any."

"In our lands they give trouble by protesting against war and executions." I remembered a bitter freezing morning in Salisbury and myself punished as an Acolyte who had disgraced the Seers' cloth. "Even against men being put into the stocks."

"They make no protests here," Cymru said. "And their Christmas worshiping is worth attending for the music."

So I walked beside him from the palace to the Cathedral. Snow fell lightly and it was cold in the open when one had become used to the heated floors of the palace, but we were well wrapped in furs. So too, I saw, were the Christians. They looked fat and prosperous, quite different from the ragged starvelings I had known in the south. There were fewer than a hundred of them. I said to Cymru:

"Is this their full number?"

"All who can will attend the Christmas worship," he said. "Their numbers dwindle.

Forty years ago, when I walked here beside my father, there were three times as many. But their music is still excellent."

Listening, I supposed it was. I found it florid stuff, with much contrast between boys' trebles and deep booming basses: there were almost as many in the choir as in the audience. But I knew nothing of music, anyway. I let my mind wander to watch the others in the church. Sitting on their high-backed benches they looked even fatter and richer than before. I wondered what our Winchester Bishop would make of them. They looked far worthier citizens than his own rabble. And yet, Cymru had said, their numbers dwindled. It was not easy to account for it.

I put the question to their Bishop later, when he came to the feast at the palace. His name was Griffis and I had seen him at court before. For such visits he put off his Christian robes and his elegance outdid the majority of Cymru's nobles, a notable achievement. He spoke elegantly too; more slowly than was usual among the Wilsh and with what was thought to be great wit. I could not always see the jest myself, but the Wilsh nobles round him were quick to laugh.

He said: "Numbers do not of themselves give distinction." From a tray proffered by a page he took a small roast bird and crunched it delicately. "It is sometimes an honor to be part of a minority." He glanced sideways at me, smiling. "Did you not find yourself in this case with the Captains of your city?"

Someone tittered. I had heard this Bishop on other occasions dripping malice from his slightly twisted mouth. The Wilsh nobles were nearly all gossips, but he outdid them in that also. I said coldly:

"You have a merry wit, Bishop." He inclined his head, smiling still. "I must tell the King that you find treachery a good subject for jesting. Maybe he will laugh with you."

He looked at me quickly to see if I were jesting in my turn. When I stared heavily back at him he quickly changed his tune. I had misunderstood him, he said, but it was for him to apologize for the misunderstanding. From that he went on fulsomely in flattery of me. It was laid on like the grease which still rimmed his lips from the bird he had been eating, smooth and oily. After a moment or two I nodded, and turned my back. It was discourtesy, but I could stand no more of the man.

I thought of the Bishop of Winchester, talking boldly about forbidden things, speaking up to an Acolyte in the presence of his Prince. And thinking of it I thought of who else had been there that night, saw her again scolding me and then sweetly pleading as she told me whom she had asked to dine with us. And sickness filled my heart as the Wilsh nobles chattered and laughed and gorged themselves all round me. I left the room and went up to the quiet of my chamber. The double windows were shut. I opened them and stepped out onto the balcony. The river was frozen except where it tumbled down its horseshoe falls, barely visible in the darkness. Beyond its lights flickered from the hundred towers of Klan Gothlen, and whispers of music came in on the night air.

The cold was sharp against my skin and memory a knife in my mind. I clenched the freezing balustrade with my fingers. Soon, thanks be to the Great, the feasting days would be over and it would be time to work again.

At last winter ended, and the army could ride south. We set off with banners and pennants flying in a stiff breeze that blew down from the mountains and still had ice in it. The citizens cheered us from their towers and balconies and thronged the streets to watch us pass. Apart from the scouts, Cymru rode in the van and I beside him.

It was a leisurely progress. We could not

travel at any great pace because of the baggage train, which was enormous. I had been for reducing it to the minimum, but on this one point Cymru overrode me. So we went laden with gear of all kinds—tents for the nobles, a pavilion for Cymru himself—and a great store of food and drink. This at least we consumed as we made our way south. But we still took far more than an army in the field needed—and far more, as I pointed out to Cymru, than we should be able to take with us over the pass through the Burning Lands.

We were sitting in his pavilion which had been set up close by the river. Our camp stretched for half a mile along the valley. Had there been any possible enemy I would have wanted it more tightly disposed, but on this side of the Burning Lands there was none to challenge the might of Cymru's army.

Cymru laughed. "We shall travel lightly when we need to, Luke, but until the need arises we Wilsh will have our comforts. Could Lewin have prepared a dinner such as we had tonight without his mountain of pots and pans and his own army of scullions?"

I said: "The contrast may come hard."

He smiled at me strangely. "You do not understand us yet. We are a people of contrasts." He looked across the river. "A people who smile and talk lightly, but our hearts are extreme."

In love and hatred I thought, but did not say. We did not talk of her but her presence was between us.

"You do not understand us, Luke," Cymru said, "but perhaps you are more like us than you think."

Bats swooped low in the dusk over the hurrying waters. We sat in silence as the night came on.

We passed the place where the polyhounds had surrounded Hans and me, and the valley of the Tribe. I wondered if Jok and the others were watching our progress from cover; I saw no sign of them. We passed the village of the building rats, deserted still and almost overgrown with weeds and saplings, and that other village from which I had been taken, as as a sacrificial victim, to the Eyrie of the Sky People. We skirted the forest in which Edmund and I, in an upper room of a crumbling palace, had found a skeleton dressed in the moldering clothes of the past, and a gold box, and a painting of an old man, done with a skill no painter of our time could equal. And so we came at last to the black desolation where trees and plants withered in the heat, where there were only rocks and steaming pools, and the air was choked with dust from the clouds of smoke that hung over the jagged peaks of the Burning Lands.

We left the baggage train there, along with Lewin and his scullions. The horses' legs were wrapped about with asbestos cloth, and we took nothing with us but our weapons. Cymru himself put aside his velvet cloaks and wore a leather jerkin, armored with slats of steel. I was surprised by the difference it made in him: he looked a warrior now.

I went across the pass first, leading the scouts. I had decided to bring the army over in units of twenty, to avoid confusion. It made it a long business. We had started in early morning but at nightfall a quarter of the army was still on the other side.

If we had been attacked during this maneuver we would have been massacred; but I had no fear of it. There was no dwelling within five miles of the pass; no blade of grass on which a wandering shepherd might feed his flock. There was only a barren desert with the Burning Lands between. The next day the rest of the army came over. We lost one horse that fell and threw its rider and had to be destroyed, having broken a leg. But another warrior picked up the horseman and got him across with nothing worse than a few burns.

When we had gathered our forces, we rode south. Kluellan had been in favor of taking the nearest town to use as a base, but I had vetoed it. That town was Marlborough. It was part of Oxford's kingdom and for more reasons than one I did not want to get embroiled with Oxford. So we bypassed it and made for Salisbury.

We had brought little in the way of provisions, ammunition for the guns being the more important consideration, and so we had to live off the land. The villages through which we passed were forced to give us food. In return we did them no harm. At one place there was a scuffle between one of the Wilsh soldiers and a girl. I do not know what caused it—the soldier swore his innocence—but Kluellan had him flogged on the spot.

From the moment of first contact, of course, pigeons had taken word of our presence, and it had spread far and wide by now. I knew they would have heard of it in Winchester, and wondered what Blodwen would think of my return at the head of her father's army. She and her lover might have had many laughs together during the winter, over poor banished Luke. This news would not give them much to laugh at.

We followed the Avon valley and so passed
within a few miles of Sanctuary. I did not try
to contact the High Seers. They had given me
a weapon but I had won an army myself. I no
longer needed either them or their Science.

It was while we were camped between
Sanctuary and the town of Amesbury that the
scouts brought word of an enemy. The army
of Salisbury had ridden north to challenge us.
So we prepared for battle, and the next morning fought it.

Our army numbered more than a thousand, of which three hundred were armed
with Sten guns. These left their horses tethered and advanced on foot. I watched it from
high ground, west of the river. They looked
like peasants as they walked across the green
fields, specked white and gold with buttercups
and daisies. In front of them, holding a slight
rise, the men of Salisbury sat their horses,
whose occasional snorts and whinnies came
thinly through the air. Their banners of red
and black blew bravely in a breeze from the
north. It was a fine sight. I felt my blood thrill
to it. The men on foot seemed puny in com-
parison.

The horsemen were preparing themselves
for the charge. I saw the bugler lift his instru-

ment to his lips and heard the harsh notes
blare out, my horse twitching under me at the
distant sound. For a moment, despite all I
knew of the weapon I had armed them with, I
did not believe the Wilsh footmen could
withstand their onslaught.

They moved, slowly at first but gathering
speed and momentum. I watched my own
troops and anxiously waited. The Captain
had been told to let them come to fifty yards
and then, on the command of one Captain,
fire together. They had practiced this against
their own horsemen, firing the bullets into
the ground in front of them; but practice, as
any warrior knew, was not the same as battle.
If they fired prematurely and raggedly, it was
possible that all might be lost.

But the months of drilling and discipline
brought their reward now. They stood like
rocks while the line of horsemen thundered
down. I guessed the distance separating them
as best I could. Two hundred yards, a hundred, seventy-five . . . Then the single cry:
"Fire!"—and after that not one tongueless
stammering giant but hundreds of them. The
valley rocked with the noise.

And as though they had crashed into a steel
rope, drawn across their front, the line of
horsemen stumbled and fell. Maybe a score

rode on a few more yards, ten, even twenty, and were picked off one by one. None reached the soldiers with the guns.

I raised my arm. From behind, the Wilsh horsemen charged in their turn, the footmen giving way to let them through. Their swords flashed as they rode down on those men of Salisbury who had risen from their dead or dying horses. Some did their best to fight, but their case was helpless. They were cut down with scarcely more trouble than a girl might take to pluck a flower. Soon they dropped their swords in surrender. From the bugle call to this instant, no more than ten minutes had passed.

Within an hour I had a visitor. He came from the north with a single troop of horse, no more than thirty men. His standard bearer carried the white flag of truce. It was Eric of Oxford.

He dismounted and gave me greeting, and I returned it.

He said: "I had news of your coming, Luke. And news earlier of what happened in Winchester. Why did you not come to me? I would have helped you."

"Your father might not have made me welcome."

"He would have known nothing." I looked

at him in inquiry. "He was gravely ill even then and confined to bed. He died in November."

"And you are Prince of Oxford? I have failed in duty."

I gave him the formal bow which a Captain should make to a ruler. He laughed.

"Enough of that! If what I hear is true you command a greater army than mine. But you may still welcome help to win back your city. I told you once: when I can help, I will. I can do so now."

"It is an army of barbarians," I said, "from beyond the Burning Lands. Have you heard that also?"

"All the more need for the support of friends! Then no one can say you required barbarians to regain your own. It looks better if you have an ally close to home. I can bring my army here within a week. Can you hold off from battle till then?"

"You are too late, Eric. The battle has been fought."

"Fought, you say?"

He looked at the bustle of the Wilsh camp around us. I said:

"And won. Would you see the field?"

He rode in silence with me. I heard him draw breath as we came in sight of the ugly rampart that marked the scene of carnage. It

was made up of the broken bodies of horses in
their hundreds, mingled with the bodies of
men. In among them moved those Wilsh I
had detailed to end the sufferings of any
horses that still lived. I think probably they
had already finished that work for no horse
moved or cried. They were engaged on a
more congenial occupation: stripping the
dead warriors of Salisbury of their rings and
ornaments.

Some ten yards from the wall of horror,
Eric reined in.

"I have never seen slaughter approaching
this," he said. "What casualties did your
Wilsh have?"

"None. None serious, at least. A few have
minor wounds."

He shook his head. "It is beyond believing.
It is said the Spirits protect you. But do they
rain death from the skies on armies that take
the field against you?"

I told him of the Sten guns. I did not say
where they came from, leaving him to think it
was a device of the Wilsh. He said:

"They are machines, then."

I asked: "Is that so hard a thing to hear, for
one who told me he looked for change from
old and stupid ways?"

"I looked for change; not for a rotting
mountain of dead horses. Your enemies are

men. Did you need to have your soldiers kill these poor beasts so mercilessly?"

"The horses are a bigger target, their riders helpless once they are brought down. The soldiers fired at them by my command. These are the right tactics for winning a battle with such a weapon."

"I believe you. But is there honor in such a victory?"

"What is honor?" I said. "They stripped mine from me in Harding's house, sitting round an oak table. But I live, to take my revenge."

Eric was silent, staring at the carnage. Directly opposite us a stallion, a magnificent bay, thrust its head upward to the sky, jaws open in a silent scream.

I said: "The old battles achieved nothing: you told me that in Winchester. They had horses and honor but they brought no resolution. Things will be different from now on. There will be no room for horses or honor in the battles we shall fight, but we shall have victories of a kind men have not known before."

Eric turned his horse's head away. He said:

"All this may well be true. I bid you farewell, then, Luke."

"You will not bring your army south to join us?"

He smiled. "I was mistaken. You have no need of help."

"And the alliance you offered me?"

"Farewell, Luke."

I rode with him a little way. "Will you fight against me?"

"Am I a fool?" he said. "I have seen your victory."

9

The Walls of Winchester

Salisbury opened its gates to us in shock. I put a garrison there and moved on. I left forty men and that was more than was needed; because I left twenty Sten guns with them. I had no fear of an uprising after the army had gone.

We took the road to the east. I had not intended to attack Romsey but their army came on us as we crossed the valley of the Test. They aimed to take us by surprise, riding out of the shelter of woods as we approached the river and clearly hoping to drive us into it.

They appeared to have some success at the outset. Their charge broke through our flank, and I heard their cry of triumph: "Romsey! Romsey!" But the flank had given way on my instructions. Our Sten gun troops were in the center. They had no time to dismount, but they wreaked a fair havoc from horseback. The attack crumpled and broke. Those that were not brought down scattered and fled to the woods from which they had started.

Our own horsemen pursued them, killing many, but I called them back by bugle. The victory was decisive enough; and a rabble fleeing back to the city served us better than unnecessary slaughter. It would be easy enough to take Romsey; and other things came first. The road to Winchester lay open.

The banners of the army that rode out of the woods had all been yellow and black and there were no men of Winchester among the fallen. This meant that Romsey had freed itself, or been set free by Harding and the rest. But although they must have heard by now how we had destroyed the army of Salisbury, they had still ridden against us alone rather than wait and join with Winchester.

Cymru spoke of it. "These are a strange people. Out of resentment, you think? But we are foreign and invade their lands. Does it not make sense to combine together when there is a threat to all?"

I tried to explain the way of it to him, but with small success. He could not conceive what it might be like to live as a citizen of one free and independent city amongst many, to nourish rivalries through generations. He came after all from a single city, an oasis of culture and prosperity surrounded by lands that were savage but offered no threat. There were no divisions among the Wilsh, or none that mattered.

Cymru shrugged. "Well, it serves our purpose. Though if all their cities sent their armies against us together, I do not think it would make much difference. This is a mighty weapon you have given us, Luke."

I looked at the mound of death beside the river.

"Mighty indeed. Nothing can stand against it."

"I have one regret."

"What is that?"

"That we lose you when you regain your city."

He had said fulsome things about me in the past, as the Wilsh commonly did; but now he spoke from the heart.

I said: "There will be commerce between us. I shall visit you in Klan Gothlen."

Cymru shook his head. "It is a long journey. And you will be well occupied here. But no man may command another's destiny. It is enough that we share this mission. We shall take your city for you and avenge the insult that concerns us both."

It was raining as we came down into the Itchen valley, a feathery drifting rain that slowly soaked to the skin. We rode past the water meadows where on a summer's day—so long ago but less than a year gone by— Edmund had played the lute and sung to Blodwen while I rode from them, foolishly content. Now the fine rain washed over the grass under a weeping sky of gray.

Our scouts reported the army of Winchester ahead of us. They had drawn up west of the river in ordinary battle array. I said to the scout who told me:

"Are you sure of this? Their full army?"

"We have covered the ground well, Lord. I think if there was a single man in hiding we would have found him."

I did not doubt it: the Wilsh made cunning scouts. Still it was hard to believe. They would have heard what happened to the warriors of Salisbury and Romsey. Surely they were not such fools as to stand in the open and wait for us to attack?

And yet when we came within view of them my heart was moved by the sight. The troops were set out in classic fashion, each with its banner of blue and gold: Captains, standard-bearers, lancers with their spears at rest, and behind them the swordsmen. It was a brave challenge to those who came against them—a challenge to battle in the old way, right arm against right arm, steel against steel: honor an equal prize with victory.

For a moment I was tempted to accept it, and to lead my Wilsh horsemen into the charge. But too many things had happened, and too much was at stake. I kept the horsemen back. The Sten gunners were already quietly moving into position on high ground to the east. One of the high-roads of our ancestors ran there. It had been a railway once and steam engines had pulled carriages along it, taking people to far places at many times the speed of a galloping horse. Now it was overgrown with bushes and trees, and gave good cover.

They could still have attacked us while the Sten gunners were taking up their places. It would have made no difference in the end, but as with the men of Romsey they might have gained an advantage at the start. But they did not move. They were waiting until our own disposition was complete. According to custom we should sound a bugle to show our readiness. Then they would attack.

Why did they do this? I wondered. Out of

folly? It might be so, but they were men I knew, and knew to be hardheaded. Nor could I think they would really believe that I would accept the challenge to fight on equal terms. If I had not spared Salisbury and Romsey, who had done me no real harm, why should I spare them?

I think it was more from resignation and despair. They could see nothing facing them except defeat; but at least they would go down in ancient fashion, fighting as the armies of Winchester had fought for generations. Perhaps it was folly, but it had grandeur in it.

My Sten gunners were ready. I made a sign to the bugler. He sounded the call and it was answered. A quarter of a mile away the line of horsemen began to move toward us.

This time I had told the Sten gunners to hold their fire until a command from me, as shown by a second blast on the bugle. The bugler rode at my side, ready for my word. In front of us the line came on, through the drizzling rain; from a walk to a canter and so to full gallop.

When they were a hundred yards from us they would be not much more than fifty yards from the gunners, thereafter moving away from them as they closed with us. It was that moment I was waiting for. I watched the distance narrow, the word ready in my mouth. When the line drew level with that stunted tree . . . I knew it well, had climbed it as a boy. The horsemen thundered on. They approached the tree; they reached it. I tried to cry my order. Ice blocked my throat and would let no word pass.

They rode in savage fury and their battle cries shattered the sky. I tried to speak again, and failed again. If they smashed into us with this impetus the Wilsh, I knew, would not withstand them: no horsemen could. Even at that moment I felt a pride in them.

They were not much more than fifty yards away. I could see the faces of men I knew: Blaine, Nicoll, Stuart. And in the center, mouth open in a yell, Edmund, who had been my friend. It was then that the ice cracked. I spoke, and the bugler blew, and at the first savage note my tongueless giants stammered out their hate.

Dozens fell but the rest came on. The guns could only fire for a few moments or they would rake us too. The line was full of gaps but it reached us. Then everything was forgotten in the clash of sword on sword.

I remember little of the battle itself. I do not know who I struck down, nor how many, nor who it was that gave me the thrust in the shoulder that all but unhorsed me. I do not know how long it lasted. Time has no meaning in a battle and this was a battle of the old kind, the last such there would ever be. All was slash and counterslash, cries of men in pain or triumph, the snort and squeal of horses, nerve-wrenching scrape and clang of steel, the wetness of rain and sweat and blood . . .

They drew back at last. Late though the command had been, the guns had taken dire toll of them before they reached us. Only desperate courage had enabled them to come to grips with our horsemen after that. They broke and scattered and fled under the shoulder of Catherine's Hill to the distant East Gate.

I did not take my men and ride after them, but let them go.

The surgeon came to see to my wound. I told him it would wait, dismissing him with anger when he persisted. I walked between the bodies of the fallen. Some of the Wilsh were unfamiliar to me but there was not a face among the Winchester I did not know. Barnes I saw, and the trooper who had taken my arm when he arrested me in my brother's name. Foster, whom Hans had come near killing in the barracks on the night of the victory feast, lay sprawled on his back—now truly dead. I saw Edmund's brother, Charles, with his head in a bloody puddle, eyes staring in surprise.

And I saw Harding. There was no mark on him, either of bullet or sword, but his horse lay dead of bullet wounds beside him. Harding's head drooped at an unlikely angle. He had been thrown when his horse fell, I guessed, and broken his neck. I looked long at him. He had always been a slight man and now seemed very small, a child grown old. I felt no pity, but no joy either.

There was another body near. A bullet had caught him high up on the forehead, making a single blackened hole through which his life had ebbed. It was Wilson, my father's oldest companion, who had refused a Captaincy from him but taken it from me; not because he wanted the honor but to protect me better. Wilson, the one Captain who had voted against the rest when they condemned me to exile.

I looked and turned away. I would have howled like a dog but the ice was back in my throat. I stumbled through the rain to where Cymru and the surgeon waited.

Greene and Ripon were two of the three who came to parley: the third was Edmund.

I received them sitting beside Cymru, with

Snake in attendance also. I offered them cakes and ale.

"It is a good brew," I said. "It was made on my father's farm, not half a mile from here. But I can give you ale from your own farms if you would prefer it."

"We want no ale," Greene said. "We seek to know your terms."

"That is easily done. I want nothing but my own: my city and the bride who was given to me by this her father."

"A city is not something that can be given," Greene said, "except by the will of its citizens. This is well known in civilized lands. Your father first seduced us from that course by taking Petersfield, and under your rule we strayed still further into error. We are paying for it now and know we must pay heavily. But we will not yield our freedom."

Cymru said: "And my daughter? Will you yield her, to her father?"

It was Edmund who answered. "A free lady may not be given up, any more than a city may. If she wishes to come to you, she will. No one will force her."

Cymru stared at him with black anger. "Your comrade talks of seducing, but what of you? You, who ate my bread, seduced my daughter from your Prince and friend. And do you chatter now of freedom?"

Greene said: "This gets us nowhere. We acknowledge defeat. We will say nothing of the way the victory was won. We will pay you gold—all the gold we have in the city. Our wives will strip the rings from their fingers to give you. Take your ransom and let us live in peace."

I shook my head. "We want no gold. No more than the gates of the city. One gate will do. And the Lady Blodwen restored to her father."

"To her father," Edmund said, "or to a man she hates?"

It told me only what I knew already but the shaft went home. The wound in my shoulder was nothing to it.

Greene said: "You will get neither. And our walls are high. Prince Stephen, Edmund's father, saw to that."

"In the end you will yield," I said. "It does not matter to us whether it is soon or late. The suffering is on your side."

"You will starve us, then?" Greene said. "We have wheat and cattle. When they have gone we will kill our horses and eat them. And after that we will hunt our rats for our suppers. And after that if we must starve then starve we will. But while there is any strength in our arms you will not come into the city."

"Brave words," I said. "But the promise is easier made than kept."

They were ready to go. Cymru said to Edmund:

"A message for my daughter."

"What is it, sire?"

"Send her her father's curse."

Edmund bowed. "She is too gentle to return it to you. But I do it for her."

They sent the Wilsh soldiers who had been Blodwen's bodyguard out to us. We kept the siege all summer. Kluellan, guided by Snake, proved an excellent quartermaster. We fed off the city farms first; then sent our troops to forage far afield. It was still no easy life, especially compared with the luxury of Klan Gothlen, and I was surprised by how well Cymru and the Wilsh nobles endured it. I had thought there might be mutterings, talk of abandoning it all, but there was none.

Much hung on Cymru himself of course, and his purpose did not waver. When I spoke of it once, he said:

"We have come a long way, Luke. Too far to abandon a purpose so nearly won."

If the paralysis had not gripped my throat when the command to fire was needed, or if I had pursued them as they fled toward the East Gate, our victory would have been sealed already. We both knew that but he had never charged me with it. I said:

"They are a stubborn people, sire."

Cymru laughed. "We Wilsh can be stubborn, too! And this hard life does us good. We have had too soft a time of it in the past."

But all the same I brooded unhappily on the future. We could not keep the army in the field in winter. It was true we had a base in Salisbury on which we could fall back; but that would be a retreat and the thought sickened me. Nor was I confident, however high their morale stayed at present, that the Wilsh would cheerfully endure a winter in a foreign city, with the prospect of resuming the siege of another foreign city in the spring. A soldier must leave home and family when his monarch requires it; but it does not mean that he forgets them. And his longing for them does not weaken with absence but grows stronger.

Then one day in late summer a man in black robes, on a white horse, rode into the camp. It was Murphy, the High Seer.

He greeted me, and said: "You look well, Luke. Older and tougher, but well. And this is the army which you abandoned us to find. We have heard great things of it. I once doubted that you would take a Wilsh army against your own city and with such weapons as we gave you. I am glad to find I was wrong."

I shrugged. "We have come so far, but here we stay. You can kill men in the field with Sten guns, but they do little harm to the stone walls of a city."

"You should have asked us for another weapon, then."

I looked at him sharply. "Is there such? Big guns, you mean? But can they be made with the materials we have?"

"No," Murphy said, "or at least not easily. But there is a thing called a mortar. It was devised for use against forts, as a siege weapon. It throws bombs at a high angle to explode against the walls."

I said doubtfully: "The walls of Winchester are not only high but strongly made."

"Have you seen a thrush with a snail?" Murphy asked. "It will pick the shell up and throw it against a stone. The shell does not break at that first impact. But the bird picks it up and throws it again. It will throw it a score of times, fifty if necessary. In the end the shell is weakened. It breaks and the thrush gets its reward. We have many more than fifty bombs for you. I promise you: the walls of the city will crack like the snail's shell."

I said: "Where is this mortar, Murphy?"

He smiled. "You will not have long to wait.

It will be here tomorrow. I rode ahead to tell you of it."

"Get me this city," I said, "and you will have your Science back. I promise that."

"Within two days it will be yours."

The mortar came at noon the next day, on a cart drawn by two horses. It was not at all like the cannons which the Prince of Petersfield had used against my father's army. They had been long and slender of muzzle. The mortar was a squat affair, wide-mouthed, almost as broad across as it was long. It looked a poor instrument to break down the walls which Stephen had spent five years building up.

And the first bomb it cast fell short, dropping in marshy ground beneath the city's wall, throwing up mud and water but doing no harm except to the frogs that dwelt there. Robb and Gunter had brought it, and they and Murphy consulted together and shifted the angle of the muzzle. The second bomb burst halfway up the wall, and the Wilsh who were watching raised a cheer at the sight. It died as the smoke cleared away, showing the wall undamaged.

The High Seers adjusted the muzzle again. The third bomb struck high up, just under the parapet. Robb said with satisfaction:

"I think we have it."

Murphy had brought field glasses with him. These had lenses like spectacles but the lenses were doubled and much stronger. They made small distant objects seem large and close. I was using them, and I said:

"There is no damage there."

"Not yet," Murphy said. "It is a lucky thrush that gets its snail at the first blow. But we have the range and it is only a question of time."

The mortar boomed again, and went on booming. After about an hour the glasses showed cracks and pittings in the wall. After two hours the parapet above that point collapsed, and the Wilsh cheered again.

The afternoon had turned warm, and the mortar itself gave off heat. Murphy wiped sweat from his brow.

"You were right. The walls are strong. But we have made a breach. Now it is only a question of hammering away at it."

"How long, do you think?"

"Not today. But by noon tomorrow there will be a hole you can take your army through."

"I can wait for that," I said.

The angle of the muzzle had to be adjusted as the breach in the wall widened and deepened. The bombardment went on until the light failed with dusk. The top half of the wall had collapsed by then, but the lower half still held.

In the morning Hans came to my tent as usual to wake me, but I was awake already. He stood in the opening, silhouetted against the faint light of dawn. I said:

"This is a good day, Hans. Today we shall see our homes again."

"Yes, sire," he said. "Sire, there is someone who would see you; from the city."

"Another deputation?" I stood up, yawning. "They are early risers. But they will get no better terms for that."

"One man only. He who was an Acolyte."

"Who was . . . ?"

I left the tent. Martin stood there, waiting. He had grown his hair and he wore ordinary clothes instead of the Acolyte's black robe. Apart from that he seemed little different. He was thin, but he had never had much flesh on his bones.

I clasped his hand and said:

"Martin! I am glad to see you. How did you get here?"

"Through the Christians' tunnel under the walls."

That was the tunnel my brother Peter had used to take the city back from the Romsey army. I had not attempted to use it because it was known now, and they could pick my men off one by one as they came out. But I had not blocked it either.

I said: "You have been in the city? I thought you went to the High Seers in the Sanctuary under the ruins of London?"

"I went there, but did not stay."

"Could they not give you what you were seeking, either?"

"No." He smiled. "I went a long journey and found what I sought in the place from which I started. But maybe the journey was necessary for all that."

"What did you find?"

"Truth. The truth that is my truth. I am a Christian, Luke."

I stared and laughed. "You jest! The truth you looked for was the truth of Science. Do you remember the old book you showed me, under the Ruins, with pictures of machines, and how bitterly you spoke against superstition and lies? Do you remember how you pleaded with me to flee the city with Ezzard, so that the mission of the High Seers could be preserved and Science at last brought back? Will you tell me now that you believe in this tale of a god born in a stable, out of the body of a maiden, who walked the earth performing wonders such as the Seers work in the

Seance Hall, who died on a cross but three days later walked again, and who at last rose into the sky to sit among the stars and judge all men? Will you tell me this?"

"All that and more. Because Science gave no meaning to my life, but this does. But I did not come here to talk of Christian beliefs, Luke. I come to plead for the city which bore us both."

"Do you? Who sent you—Edmund, who stole my lady from me, and then the city itself?"

I spoke bitterly. Martin shook his head.

"I have not seen them, except at a distance. Would a noble send a Christian to plead on his behalf? I can tell you they are thin from hunger. There is no one in the city who is not. There has been great suffering, Luke."

"If there has been suffering it was freely chosen. It does not take much to open a gate."

"If tyranny is waiting to come in, it does."

"Do you call me tyrant?"

"Whoever takes what a man will not freely give is that. A tyrant or a thief."

"You use harsh words, old friend," I said. "This thief, this tyrant, once saved you when you hung in chains, awaiting death by fire."

"Yes. For that, you may demand anything of me. But not of the city."

There was a sharpness in the air, almost of

frost. Summer was giving way to autumn. Winter would follow soon.

I said: "The suffering is almost at an end. I do not need a gate to be opened now. Before the day is over my soldiers will walk through the shattered wall into the streets of Winchester. Or will your stable-god who worked such miracles work one here?"

"It may be. Through the weak bodies of his servants."

I laughed. "The Christians will build the wall again? I do not think they can build as fast as my mortar breaks it down."

Martin took off his spectacles and wiped his eyes. I saw that his hand trembled.

"You are not a cruel man, Luke," he said. "Only blind. If you could see them starving, all those you knew—men and women, dwarf and human and polymuf—you would have pity. No, do not say it. They have only to open a gate. They can get bread in exchange for freedom. And meanwhile they are behind walls and you do not see them. But we will make you see."

"You waste your time," I said. "It is almost over. And I have won."

"Not yet." He pushed the spectacles back onto his nose. "I said the truth I have found gives a meaning to life. To death, also. I will leave you now. When I return to the city I will stand in the breach of the wall. I fear the thought as much as any man would, maybe more than most, but I think God will give me strength. Your bombs will shatter flesh and bone as well as stone." He smiled. "You have reminded me that I owe you a death. I am glad to repay it in this fashion."

"You speak bravely," I said, "and I believe that you would do it, with or without the help of your god. But I win here also. I have guards within call. You will not go back to the city until I am master of it."

"Imprison me if you wish," Martin said. "It makes no difference. I was sent here because I was your friend. There are others who will do this task, many others. The High Seers have brought you field glasses, I see, as well as a mortar. Use them to look at the wall."

The light was feeble still. With the naked eye one saw only the wall's gray shape, with the ragged V where the mortar bombs had crumbled it. But the glasses showed me other things. Small figures stood in the embrasure or clung to the broken edges of the wall. I counted a score of them, and more. I thought I saw the bald head of the Bishop. I remembered his words in Blodwen's apartment:

"If killing there must be I would rather it

were done by a warrior who kills with his own hand, and knows what bloody corpse he leaves behind."

While I watched they began singing. One of their dirge-like hymns; it sifted thinly down through the cold dawn air.

"Give the order to fire whenever you choose," Martin said. "But this time you will not be blind. This time you will see what it is you do."

Men came from their tents, attracted by the singing. Cymru and Snake and Kluellan came to me, and the High Seers. They watched the singing Christians in the breach, and watched me also. Other figures appeared on top of the walls. They lined the parapets, in scores, in hundreds. There were not so many Christians in Winchester. These were the people of the city, human and dwarf and polymuf, offering their bodies as its bulwark.

I said to Martin: "Go back to them. Tell them they can keep their freedom."

10

The Sword
of the Spirits

In sleep last night I was in Winchester. I dreamed of an afternoon when Edmund and Martin and I climbed Catherine's Hill together, with the sun burning out of blue gulfs of sky and the clouds huge and white and slow-sailing. We had taken nets with us to catch butterflies, but all we saw were cabbage whites which were not worth taking. So we lay on the grass, under the shade of the trees which cover the hilltop, and talked idly as boys will talk on hot summer days: of dreams and hopes and nonsense. And when it was time to go home for tea we started down the hill, and Edmund cried: "Race you to the bottom!" and we began to run. Edmund and I left Martin behind and Edmund began to outdistance me also. So I ran faster and faster, taking giant strides, and then as the descent grew steeper I was skipping over the grass, unable to stop or check myself, until my feet left the ground altogether and I cartwheeled through the air, and the whole earth seemed to rise up and crash against me.

All this was as it happened. I remembered lying on the ground, dazed, my head throbbing savagely with pain, and Edmund and Martin coming to pick me up. I remembered the concern in their faces and even the shirt Edmund was wearing, blue with a patch at the elbow.

But there the dream changed. I was in bed and smarting from different wounds—the burns I got in my struggle with the Bayemot. And Blodwen stood by me, in her dress that was the color of beech leaves in winter. She took my bandaged hand and said: "You are a fool, Luke. But very brave . . ." She said: "There is to be a banquet where my father will give you a great honor. A prize. Do you want to know what prize it is, brave, foolish Luke?" She leaned forward, laughing, her golden hair falling almost to touch my face. "A prize . . . ," she whispered.

My heart was open and easy. In my dream I said what I had never been able to say in life:

"I love you, Blodwen."

As I spoke the words she drifted from me. I

called after her and she smiled and shook her head. I tried to rise and follow, but could not. Her figure faded in the distance, and I awoke and found my pillow wet with tears, and the high towers of Klan Gothlen framed in the window opposite my bed.

It is three years since I led the army of the Wilsh back across the Burning Lands. Cymru calls me his son. He governs in name but leaves the exercise of authority to me. I am to be Cymru after him, and the people applaud this. Although a foreigner, I am their hero. The great painting of Luke and the Bayemot covers one wall of the throne room, and Gwulum and his apprentice artists have nearly finished the other one that faces it. It is called "The Conquest of the South" and shows me at Cymru's side in the Battle of the Itchen. My sword is raised to strike down a Captain who menaces him.

The High Seers came with us to Klan Gothlen. They do not call themselves High Seers any longer and do not practice mumbo jumbo and give messages from the Spirits in darkened halls. They are scientists. They have set up schools and a university, at which the ancient knowledge is freely taught.

The Wilsh take gladly to this learning. Almost every day, it seems, there are new machines and devices to change our way of life. Last week a motor car chugged uneasily along the main street of the city, to the cheers of the onlookers. There is talk of building a railway to make easier our conquest and development of the savage lands. As soon as the engineers can make up their minds as to whether it will be twin-rail or monorail, the project will be put underway.

My people are happy and contented. Snake is a good Chancellor and Kluellan keeps the army at a high pitch of ceremonial drill: there is no real need for anything else. Hans is busily occupied with this notion of a railway. He has married a girl of human stock, though not much taller than he is, and they have a human child, a daughter.

Our local Christians still sing well, and their numbers still dwindle. The Bishop, who comes often to the palace and whom I have learned to tolerate—he has a sharp wit after all—is enthusiastic for Science. He has even written a book, extolling its spiritual values.

Our writ runs, with increasing sureness, to the edge of the Burning Lands. We have no contact with the parts beyond. Not long after our return a small eruption sealed the pass. This is a temporary thing—the scientists say the volcanoes are dying down—but it has cut us off from the south.

I am glad of it, though the isolation cannot last. Even if the pass stays closed there are other ways of meeting. There is a town being built by the sea at the mouth of the River Mawddach, under the shadow of Cader Idris, and ships big enough to be safe from any Bayemot will go out from there. In a few years we shall have flying machines as well. The Burning Lands will offer no barrier.

So we shall meet with the cities of the south again, and when we do we shall conquer them. It will not serve them to line their walls with the living bodies of their citizens. We shall have weapons more subtle and more powerful than Sten guns and mortars: weapons of ease and novelty and riches. We shall conquer them because we represent the strength of the future, and they the past which must always bow to it. It will happen because it must, but I am in no great hurry to see it.

I am content here much of the time. I busy myself with work and government. It is the hours of idleness that chafe. Cymru would have me marry and the Wilsh nobles tempt me with their daughters. They are pretty enough, some of them beautiful, but they do not move me.

The Sword of the Spirits lies in a golden casket in the throne room. Swords have no use any longer, though there was a fashion last winter of wearing ornamental daggers, but this one is treasured for its history and will be as long as the towers of Klan Gothlen stand and Cymru rules there. It is a trophy, a legacy, that a man would be glad to leave to his son.

But I shall have no son.